Kingston to Cable

Kingston to Cable

Gary Greenwood

First Published in 2011 by
Pendragon Press
Po Box 12, Maesteg, Mid Glamorgan
South Wales, CF34 0XG, UK

ISBN 978 1 906864 21 7

Typeset by Christopher Teague

Printed and Bound in Wales by
MWL Digital Print, Pontypool

www.pendragonpress.net

This one is for

Rich H, Dave B and Sean Q

who walked a strange Land and showed me what lay within

For we are Strangers before thee, and sojourners, as were all our fathers: our days on the earth are as a shadow, and there is none abiding.

I Chronicles, Ch 29, v 15

Author's Foreword

There's a certain type of reader who will take the time to read a book's foreword before reading the actual story. Most readers I have encountered are happy to just dive straight into the story and will, at best, skim a foreword if not ignore it altogether – it's the story they're interested in, after all, not the inane ramblings of someone talking about the story.

If you're reading this after you've finished *Kingston To Cable*, I hope you enjoyed it and that the shifts in narrative weren't confusing. If you're about to start the story but have taken a moment to read this foreword first, I promise I'll be brief so you can get on with the book.

Kingston To Cable is made up of nine stories that form one complete tale; those stories were written intermittently between 1990 and 2007 which is a long old time for a story that reaches around 60,000 words - I know authors who can do that amount in a few weeks. The first story, *Kingston*, was the first short story I ever had published outside of a competition and I thank Mike Chinn, then editor of *Mystique: Tales of Wonder* for both accepting it and coining the phrase "spaghetti fantasy" to describe it. The other stories came about one after another over the intervening years and for a long time the tale finished at what is now *The End, For Now* in a slightly experimental way . . . which is to say it didn't really end at all. Eventually I submitted the whole thing to Chris Teague at Pendragon Press and he, rightly so as it turned out, told me to stop being a pretentious git and write a real ending. This coincided with Mark Chadbourn telling me he'd gone back to writing with pen and paper; taking my cue from him I did the same and, in a relatively short amount of time, wrote the last two stories, *Still Waters* and *Cable*, so thanks to Mark as well.

As the stories were written independently of each other, the narrative changes throughout the tale. Most of it is in the third person but the first, third, much of the fifth and the last stories are all in the first person, and all different first persons on top of that. You're all readers so I'm sure you can cope with that.

The mixture of a pseudo-Old West setting and a fantasy world where magic and wizards exist will obviously encourage comparisons with Stephen King's masterpiece, *The Dark Tower* and it would be pointless to deny a lack of influence, though you'll find no *kas* or *kennets* here, *thankee sai* very much. *The Dark Tower* books are superb (though I still disagree with the almost criminal way King discarded Flagg) but *Kingston To Cable* grew from a lot more than them, first and foremost the Dungeons and Dragons games that myself and my friends played when we were about 15 or 16. The characters of Hook, Saxon and Dale that you'll meet in the stories wouldn't have existed were it not for Rich Hayward, Dave Bull and Sean Quarterly - while the characters I've created aren't the same as those my friends guided around my fantasy world of Aym (usually sitting in Dave's front room) there's enough there to warrant the dedication of this book to the three of them. The other major influence on the story stems from another shared love we all had at the time and, to greater or lesser extents, still do: the lyrics and music of the late Ronnie James Dio, from his days in Rainbow, through Black Sabbath and his solo band Dio. Eagle eyed readers with a knowledge of his work will find more than one reference to the man and his songs scattered throughout the story.

Over all, however, it's the Western genre, both in books and films, that drove *Kingston* to finally get to *Cable*. My grandfather introduced me to Western novels as a small boy, lending me books by J T Edson, George G Gilman and the ubiquitous Louis L'Amour and I devoured them as quickly as I could. Later, I would watch Western films with him - there always seemed to be a black and white Western on TV on a Saturday or Sunday afternoon in those days - but while he favoured John Wayne, it was the grimmer and grittier Clint Eastwood that I was drawn to. While I've often said that *Star Wars* is as close as I get to a religion, Sergio Leone's Dollars trilogy of *A Fistful Of Dollars, For*

A Few Dollars More and my favourite film of all time, *The Good, The Bad And The Ugly* had a greater impact on me than anything else in the long run.

Which brings me to my final influence: religion. *Kingston To Cable* didn't start out as a story about gods and belief but it quickly turned out to be one . . . well, as quickly as any story that takes eighteen years to write can do. Religion has long fascinated me though I've never been a believer and it has run through a lot of my writing, in particular the novels *The King Never Dies* and *What Rough Beast*. With the whole of the Land at my disposal, I could create my own gods, allowing me to draw once more from the Dungeons and Dragons days and drop in my own favourite non-player character who surprised me by giving himself a much larger role than was first envisaged.

Anyway, I said I'd be brief and have obviously failed in that but will try and wrap things up by thanking a few people: as mentioned above, Mike Chinn, Chris Teague and Mark Chadbourn; Mark West for reading through the draft and giving me some much needed constructive criticism; Tim Lebbon, Matt Williams and Max O'Hagan for the usual reasons; the dynamic duo of Steve Lockley and Paul Lewis for organising the writers' getaways; Paul Meloy, Mark Morris, Adam Neville, Sarah Pinborough and Tim Lebbon (again) for food and beer at the getaways; the usual FantasyCon crowd of Stuart Young, Mark Samuels, Gary McMahon, Alison Davies and John Probert and anyone else I have a beer with; and, as always, my wife, Ly for putting up with so, so much from me - cheers, darling!

Now for those of you who haven't read the book yet, I hope you enjoy it. For those who have come back to this foreword after reading it, don't spoil it for those about to read it.

Cheers!

KINGSTON

"**S**tranger coming."

I sat up in my seat and looked up and down the dusty main road. Ma Berry's eyes weren't wrong, despite her being close to eighty. Up ahead, strolling into town from the East, was a Stranger, wearing a big, dark overcoat which had been painted a light brown by the dust that clung to it. Jammed on his head, keeping off the sun, was a wide brimmed black hat, just like the one Old Thomas the undertaker wore. There was no sign of guns.

"First of the Season," Ma Berry said, turning back to her knitting. I nodded, still watching the figure trudge down the street, my bottle of beer forgotten in my lap.

"Howdy," said the Stranger as he came level with us. As we were sat on the porch, he had to look up and the sun finally shone on his face. Not particularly handsome, but close enough to avoid plain, his cheeks and chin covered with a dark scrub of beard. "This Kingston?"

"Uh–huh," said Ma Berry, folding up her knitting and looking at the Stranger for the first time. "You'll be wanting the Station?"

The Stranger nodded and Ma Berry pointed down the street.

"Hitch a left by the store and it's right in front of you."

He touched the brim of his hat, said "Thank you ma'am, sir," then turned and walked off.

1

Both of us watched him walk down the empty street, deserted due to the heat of midday, until he turned left at the store.

"First of the Season," Ma Berry repeated, and again I nodded.

By the end of that week, the few children of Kingston had gone through the whole list of rumours that have built up around the Strangers, a breed of men and women who wander from one Kingdom to another. According to the children the Stranger, who gave his name as Slake, was a god, an angel, a prophet, a wizard, a demon. Chances are he was all, some or none of these – you can never tell with Strangers.

He didn't go about much during the day; he tended to stay in the Station where the Strangers lodge, but in the evenings he visited the bar, a place too small to warrant a name, where he would sit and sup a pint or two, unmindful of the gossip that was whispered about him. Strangers are tolerated, but they're never really welcome in any small Frontier town, perhaps because so many men want to be one, desiring the freedom to come and go as they please and the powers that some of them have. At least this Slake seemed to be one of the better Strangers; as in everything, there were good and bad Strangers and, as Slake kept quietly to himself, the people of Kingston were more tolerant than usual.

Then Hook turned up.

It was towards the end of the week and Ma Berry and I were sat out on her porch again, her knitting, me supping a beer, just like when Slake had arrived. Ma Berry had seen him coming in off the Potter's Fields, but this Hook fella, he just popped up at our feet, grinning at us, scaring us half to death. He swept off his hat and bowed theatrically.

"Good morning ma'am, sir," he said. "Am I right in thinking that this is Kingston?"

Ma Berry was silent. She knitted furiously, the needles clacking rapidly together, blatantly ignoring the Stranger. I always get embarrassed when forced into this position with someone I don't know, especially with a Stranger, but I leaned forward and waved my hand at him to get his attention. When he was looking at me, I nodded in answer to his question.

"Good. Which way's the Station?" he asked. I pointed down the street, and then left. "Down the street?" I nodded. "Then where?"

Again I indicated left.

"Left?" Nod. "First left?" Nod. "Say, can't you talk?" I shook my head and he smiled up at me. "Hell, ain't that something? You're pretty good," I shrugged, smiling myself. "You ought to be in a goddamn freak show, you know that? You'd make a lot of money," he chuckled, tipped his hat at us both and walked off.

Ma Berry put her knitting down and looked over at me.

"I'm sorry son, I should have dealt with him," I shrugged and looked down the street after the Stranger so she wouldn't see the tears that threatened to run down my cheeks. "He's going to be trouble," she said sagely, her knitting needles clacking together again.

Hook was indeed trouble. The first evening he was in town, he caused a fight in the bar, insinuating to Tom Dunn that he had taken his wife behind the general store that afternoon. The pair went outside, and Hook re–entered a few minutes later wiping his knuckles, a smile on his face. Several of the men looked towards Slake who was sat in a corner, perhaps expecting him to do something. We Natives are reluctant to tangle with Strangers unless we're both drunk and provoked as Tom had been, and we generally leave them to each other, as most of them do with us.

When Slake finished his pint, however, he left and went back to the Station.

I was in the bar when, a few days later, after Hook had raped three women and wrecked both his room at the Station and the front of the corner store, a group of eight or nine men got together and plucked up enough courage to confront Slake. Abe Evans walked at the front of the group, his hat clutched tightly in his hands and held to his chest, while behind him was young Jimmy Hayfield who can't have been more than seventeen. They stood by Slake's table where he sat, calmly sipping a beer, staring off into nothing.

"Mr. Slake, sir?" Abe said uncertainly. Strangers are just that, strange, and when talking to one it always pays to be courteous. You never know whether you're talking to a god or a man, although Abe certainly hoped it was the latter.

Slake turned his head and looked at the group who were mostly my age, in their mid twenties, though one or two, including Abe, were about forty.

"Yes?" he said.

"Mr. Slake, sir, me an' a couple of the men would like to ask you a favour, sir," Abe said uncertainly. Slake said nothing, merely took a sip of his beer and kept looking at them. "It's about this Mr. Hook, sir. The other Stranger in town," Abe stopped again, obviously hoping that Slake was going to say something, but it seemed the Stranger was in no mood to make things easy. "We'd like something done about him, sir. About Mr. Hook, sir."

Slake leaned back against the wall and looked at them. "So why don't you do something yourselves?" he asked. Abe and the others swapped glances. One of the older men, Bill Swithen, looked as if he was going to faint at the prospect of even talking to Hook. Jimmy Hayfield stepped forward, though, and glared at Slake.

"Why should we? He's a Stranger, like you."

"So speak to the Sheriff."

"We don't have one, Mr Slake, sir," Abe said. "Kingston ain't big enough to warrant one."

Slake smiled ruefully up at Jimmy. "Well, just tell him you want to go."

"Just like that?" Jimmy asked scornfully. Slake nodded. "And

4

what if he doesn't go? What if he kills the guy who tells him?" Abe and the others looked at each other again as if they hadn't considered violence.

Slake shrugged. "If he starts anything, then I'll help. But you have to make the first move."

"What good will your help be to the man who's dead?" Jimmy asked. Abe put his hand on Jimmy's shoulder to restrain him, but he shrugged it off. We'd never heard a Native speak to a Stranger like that before – it just didn't happen. "When are you Strangers going to start giving instead of taking?"

"When are you Natives going to stop depending on us to do your dirty work?" Slake asked, angry himself. "Every time you have some sort of problem, you either blame it on a Stranger or expect him to remedy it or both," He thumped his tankard down, spilling beer on to the table, and stood up. Everyone except Jimmy took a step back. "You can't let us get on with our lives, can you?"

"You're the ones who walk into our towns, mister," Jimmy said quietly. "We don't ask you to come, yet when there's a problem with another Stranger, none of you ever want to help," He stared up at Slake, stuck his thumbs through his belt loops and said "Why don't you get out of here?"

"And what about Hook?"

"We'll deal with him," Slake smiled at that as if he knew something we didn't, then, without taking his gaze from Jimmy, he called out to the bartender to tell him how much he owed. The barkeep, Moses Evans, Abe's younger brother, totted up some figures on a scrap of paper then shouted out "Thirteen forty six."

Slake fished in his pocket and drew out a handful of coins, sorted through them and handed twenty crowns to Jimmy.

"Go pay the bartender for me, and keep the change, kid," He smiled, patted Jimmy on the head, and left.

The Station Master confirmed it the next morning: Slake had packed up and moved on during the night, although Hook was very much still here. I've talked about that with some of the others who were in the bar at the time, and we think maybe Slake was planning to leave that night anyway. Maybe.

It didn't take long, though, for what had happened in the bar to become general knowledge. Jimmy was greeted by cheers from the children, who thought he was some kind of hero, and with jeers from the men who wanted to know just how he was going to 'deal with' Hook.

Jimmy stayed in his ma's house for the rest of that day while Hook ran riot through the town, smashing windows and the like for the Hell of it. Despite Hook's being a Stranger, there's only so far you can push people and that evening, just before I left Ma Berry's house for the bar, Abe Evans knocked for me.

"Just to let you know," he said, "there may be some trouble at the bar tonight. Some of the men . . . well, they've had enough of this Hook fella. A few of us have got together to have a word with him."

I pulled a piece of paper out of my pocket and the stub of a pencil I carry around, wrote *Jimmy?* and handed it to Abe. He laughed and gave it back.

"No, we don't expect to see Jimmy. He hasn't been out of his house all day. He's all talk."

I raised my eyebrows. What I'd seen and heard the night before hadn't been just talk.

Abe shrugged at my expression. "Maybe he will show, maybe he won't. Anyhow, just letting you know that it might not be a good idea to go to the bar tonight," He raised his hand and walked off down the porch, then turned as he heard me following.

"Where're you going?" he asked. I held up my hand to my mouth as if I had a glass and made drinking motions. He shook his head, clapped me on the back and smiled. "Sweet Judas, can't tell you anything can I?"

I shook my head, smiling, and we walked to the bar.

About fifteen minutes after Abe and I sat down with our drinks,

Jimmy came in. The whole room went silent in a second, and I thought *Christ, he's a Stranger.* Perhaps this is how Strangers are made – I don't know.

He walked up to the bar, bravely ignoring the stares of the others, and ordered a pint of beer. I found it incredible that the whole town should have turned against him in the course of one day, and for what? Saying he would deal with Hook? The men I sat with were planning to do the same thing so why was Jimmy being alienated?

I looked at him as he stood alone at the bar. His friends, Bill Swithen among them, were all sat less than three feet away, and yet they ignored him completely. I pitied him and wished to Judas I could have gone over there and talked to him.

The door opened, and Hook walked in.

"Jimmy!" he shouted. Everyone looked at Jimmy as he turned to face the Stranger who walked up to him. "My friend Slake told me you wanted a word. That right?" He leaned forward and shoved his grinning face close to Jimmy's who, although he was as white as a sheet, didn't flinch.

"Yes, I do."

"Why don't we talk about this outside, then?" He put one arm around Jimmy's shoulders and indicated the door.

"No. In here," he took Hook's arm off his shoulders. "We want you out, Hook."

"We, Jimmy?" Hook looked around the room and most of the men, myself included, would not meet his gaze. "I don't see any *we*, Jimmy. It looks as if you're on your own," Hook darted over to one of the nearby tables and snatched a pint of beer from the grasp of one of the men. He stood in front of Jimmy and took a gulp.

As he did, Jimmy hit the bottom of the tankard with his open palm, pushing it into Hook's mouth, breaking his teeth and his nose with a heavy crunch. Hook fell back, landing hard on the floor, screaming in pain and shock. Before he could move, Jimmy jumped on to his stomach, knocking the wind out of him, clutched the tankard and raised it over his head. Hook's hand shot between Jimmy's legs, grabbed and squeezed. Jimmy yelled and dropped the tankard. With casual ease, Hook pushed him off and stood up.

He looked around at all of us, blood running from his ruined mouth and nose, his eyes wild.

"Anyone else?"

Jimmy punched upward from the floor, his fist smacking hard into Hook's groin. His legs buckled and he fell forward, Jimmy rolling out of the way. He grabbed the tankard again and swung it around, this time connecting solidly with Hook's head. He struggled to his feet, giving Hook a swift kick in the ribs. Looking around at us, as Hook had done, he staggered back to the bar and leant there, gasping for breath, still cradling his groin with one hand and holding the tankard with the other.

With a groan, Hook raised himself up and turned to face Jimmy.

"You're pretty good," he said, still with that, crazy, broken smile.

"Get out of here," Jimmy panted.

Hook shook his head slowly. "Not without you, Jimmy," he said and dived low, grabbing him by the waist, Jimmy pounding on his back with the tankard. Hook pulled him away from the bar, grabbed his legs and stood up, dangling Jimmy's torso down his back with his legs straight out in front of him. He turned slowly and staggered to the door, Jimmy struggling and shouting, but never once calling for help.

Help came, however, from Abe Evans. As Hook passed our table, Abe stuck his foot out, tripping Hook and sending him crashing to the floor with Jimmy on top of him. Jimmy rolled off and on to his knees, grabbed Hook's hair with both hands and pulled his head up, then smacked it down on to the floor.

Abe suddenly stood up and grabbed one of Hook's arms. "Come on!" he called to the rest of us and soon damn near everyone in the bar had hold of some part of the Stranger. We lifted Hook bodily, him screaming and shouting all the while, out in to the street. Lights were lit in houses and people came to see what all the commotion was about. With a great cry, we threw Hook to the ground and gathered around him.

Slowly, he stood. Jimmy stepped forward into the rough circle that we had formed around him.

"We want you out, Hook. Now."

He laughed, actually laughed at us, and threw his arms wide.

"Then I shall go, dear Jimmy, but not before this —"

A circle of fire sprung up around the pair of them, shooting up to ten feet or so, making us all jump back and shield our eyes. It seemed to last hours, but could have been there no more than a few seconds before it vanished leaving a circle of ash burned into the road.

Jimmy knelt on the ground, clutching himself tightly, rocking back and fore, his clothes and hair scorched and smoking.

Hook was nowhere to be seen.

Jimmy never told us what, if anything, happened inside that circle of fire. A week later he left Kingston for good, saying he was going to hunt for Hook. We never saw him again.

We only had two more Strangers for the rest of the Season, both of them only staying a day or so, and since then we haven't seen hide nor hair of one, which suits us just fine.

None of the men ever mention Hook. I guess we're all too ashamed. Despite all of us throwing him out of the bar at the end, it took a seventeen year old kid to show us how to do it, and that's something that doesn't sit right on a lot of men's shoulders.

Old Thomas the undertaker claimed he'd seen Hook again, a few years later, still bearing the scars from his fight with Jimmy, being hunted by one of his own, another Stranger. I don't know if that's true, but if it is, I hope that Stranger caught up with Hook sooner or later and finished what Jimmy started.

EAST CAME THE STRANGER

The old woman sat in a chair in front of her small hut, gently rocking back and forth, while all around her the life of Penny's Forest went on as it had for countless years. Somewhere off to the South she heard the harsh, raucous calls of the mating wood dogs, fighting amongst themselves for the right to carry on their bloodline. To the North was the quiet stillness of the Sadducee Plains that ran on for more miles than she had ever travelled in her youth, even when she had lived and roamed with the tribes of Walkers that made the Plains their home. West of her lay the vast bulk of the Forest, populated with creatures that she had only heard in the late hours of the night, things that sounded large enough to tumble trees as they passed on their way, leaving craters in the trail roads that led to the towns and cities of the Mainland Kingdoms. And East? East came the Stranger.

She had dreamed of him for the past three nights, a Stranger unlike any that she had ever met or heard of, young and hale with a rage in his eyes that burned her dreaming mind and left after images in her sight all morning. Now he came, walking slowly, hat on his head, pack on his back, wearing no guns but with a large knife strapped to his right thigh. As she sat outside her hut, she watched him with eyes that were still keen despite the evening's approach. He strolled out of the fields that bordered this side of the Forest, and climbed over a low stone wall that had been left by empires long past. She watched him walk into the bushes and scrub at the edge of her garden, working his way through them until he stood a few feet from her home.

"Howdy, ma'am," he said, tipping his hat at her.

"Stranger," the old woman said, nodding her head by way of greeting.

"Could you tell me the quickest way through this wood?"

"Ain't no wood here, son. Them trees is Penny's Forest, leastways they have been since old man Penny went and got himself killed in 'em hundred odd year ago."

"What's the easiest way through it?" the Stranger asked again.

"What's your rush, son?" The old woman reached into the pocket of her loose dress and took out a pair of yellow apples and offered one of them to him. "Will you eat with me, Stranger?"

The Stranger looked over at the Forest and listened to the sounds that came from within, then swung his pack down to the ground. He dragged a nearby log up and sat opposite the old woman, taking the proffered apple and biting into it, not realising his thirst was so great until he felt the juice upon his tongue.

"What's your name, Stranger?"

"Justice, ma'am," he took his hat off and placed it on the ground beside him.

"That's a mighty strong name, son. You out looking to find some?"

"Something like that," the Stranger said, biting again into the apple.

The old woman sat in her chair and looked up at the sky, its blue surface lightly painted with pale grey clouds. She took an old, wooden handled knife from her pocket and sliced off a small piece of apple, popping it into her mouth and sucking noisily on it.

"I am looking for something: another Stranger. Have you seen any round these parts?"

"Happen I have. What's he look like?"

Justice thought for a while, eating his apple, then shrugged and said "Tall, over six feet. He'll probably have scars around his top lip and a broken nose. Probably lost a couple of his front teeth, too. Name's Hook."

"And what're you after this Stranger for?"

For a brief moment, Justice almost threw the last of his apple away and walked into the Forest, tired of her questions and impatient to be on his way. As quickly as his anger had risen, though, so did a lethargy and complacency settle over his bones, and he sagged on the log he was using as a seat.

"What have you done to me woman?"

"Uh—huh. Soo's apples have that effect if you ain't used to them. And nobody who thinks Penny's Forest is a wood will have met Soo's apples before, am I right or am I right, Stranger?" She sliced off another piece of apple and pushed it into her mouth chuckling. "Now; why're you after Hook?"

"You talk as though you know him. Has he asked you to waylay me?"

"No, I don't really know him," she said adjusting her position on her seat before carrying on. "I only met him about three, maybe four days ago as he came in off the fields, much the same as you, hurrying on his way. He stopped for a bite to eat, too, and I fed him a couple of them Soo's apples. He told me there was another Stranger chasing him, but he wasn't sure how far behind you were."

"Three or four days you say?" Justice sat there, the last of his apple uneaten. "I didn't realise I was so close. Was he scared?"

The old woman chuckled again, tossing the remains of her apple off to one side into the long grass. No sooner had it landed than a series of squeaks and a rush of activity was heard as something, or several things, dived upon the core and made off with it.

"He was a wicked man, but intelligent. Perhaps the worst combination you can find in a Stranger. Yes, he was scared. You're right, too, when you ask whether Hook asked me to waylay you. He wanted me to hold you here for as long as possible, and when I refused, telling him that the ways of Strangers were not mine to meddle with, he became quite angry. He very nearly overcame the Soo's apples at one point, threatening to do all sorts of things to me if I didn't help to delay you, but I stuck to my guns so to speak and told him that I would not interfere for him. Eventually, of course, I let him go and he headed off into the Forest, heading West for the Mainland Kingdoms," she paused and looked over at Justice where he sat before her. "Which is where you'll be wanting to follow him to, I guess?"

Justice nodded while trying to wake himself from the stillness the Soo's apple had induced in him.

"Why?"

He looked at her for a moment, stunned by her simple question. "I have sworn that I would search for him," he answered.

"Why?"

"He terrorised my town, and I was the only one brave enough to go up against him."

"Your town? You were a Native?" Justice nodded again. "I see. He made you into a Stranger, forced you into this . . . this quest that you are on. And what happens when you find him?"

Justice bowed his head. "He knows something I need answered. I have to find him and make him tell me."

"How long have you been chasing him?"

"Two years now."

The woman snorted derisively. "Two years and yet you still talk in generalities. You've no real idea of what happens when you find him, do you? You questers, you are all the same. Your attention is fixed solely on your object of desire, never what you have to do to get there, nor what you will do after you reach it.

"Your life at the moment, Justice, is like a straight road that has been built over everything in its path, but some way along there is a wall built across it, a wall with a door. You dimly perceive the road up to that point, taking each step as it comes. But when you reach the wall and the door, your object of desire, your meeting with Hook, until you get there you have no idea of what lays beyond it, what the future holds." She looked down her nose at him. "Why do you need to do this thing? What answer could be so important that your whole life can be changed?"

The Stranger was silent, ignoring her question.

"I will offer you the advice I have given every such blind quester that I have known: leave it. Forget your quest and get on with your life, such as it is. These things lead only to damnation. Or boredom."

They sat quietly for several minutes, only the sounds of the Forest around them. The old orange sun dipped its way towards the West, its bottom edge just above the tops of the distant trees. Mustering his strength, feeling the apple's effect waning, Justice stood carefully, picking up his pack and hat.

"Thank you for your advice, ma'am. I believe I'll be on my way now," He slipped his pack up on to his back and headed off West into Penny's Forest. She watched him for a while as he became smaller and smaller until his form was lost in the darkness beneath the branches. Reaching into her dress pocket she removed another apple and, using the knife, began to eat.

"You can come out now."

A Stranger stepped out from behind the hut into the late evening gloom and stood behind her chair. Tall, over six feet, with a fine network of scars around his mouth and nose, he placed a wide brimmed hat upon his head, a once jaunty feather now hanging limply from the band.

"You were right, then," he said.

"Did I not say I would be? This Justice, he is young and foolish. He believes only in the romance of quests and revenge, convinced you hold some answer that he must know. I am glad that you have seen fit to abandon this whole thing, Hook; go your own way, now, and try to live better than you have."

"What can I say, old woman? You have shown me the error

of my ways and I will forever be in your debt," Hook said with a smile.

"It is the least I can do. This Justice now believes you are headed West to the Mainland Kingdoms and will likely spend his whole life chasing shadows of you until he realises that he need not do it any further, or he is killed. You should go North, Hook, into the Sadducee Plains. Travel with one of the Walker tribes. The chances of his finding you in that wilderness are almost non–existent."

"Again, old woman, what can I say? I am glad that you allowed me to stay here and listen to your pleas to the boy. How can I ever thank you?"

The old woman smiled, congratulating herself. "Leave me now, and settle yourself. You can never become a Native, but at least you can stop being such a Stranger."

"Alright. I'll go now," Hook said, at the same time plunging his knife through the back of her chair and up into her heart, twisting the blade against the wood of the chair and her thin ribs, grinning as he heard both crack loudly. With a final gasp, the old woman slumped down in her seat. Pulling his knife out of her corpse, he reached over and wiped the blade clean on her dress.

"Wicked and intelligent," he said shaking his head in mock remorse. "Bad combination," Sheathing his knife, he adjusted the pack on his back and began to walk west into Penny's Forest, whistling to himself all the while.

When he had gone, the old woman coughed sending a thin shower of blood into the air that fell like a gentle rain on to her dress.

A man, tall and dressed in clothes that were made from odd patches of red and green cloth roughly sown together, stepped out from the hut. On his head he wore a three pointed hat, each point decorated with a single bell at the end that tinkled slightly as he walked.

"By all the gods that hurt," the old woman said.

"I told you it would," the man said, looking out into the forest

15

after Hook and Justice. "Still you've done your job."

"Why them –" her words were interrupted by another racking cough that sent more blood flying, this time larger lumps of crimson that splattered her clothes. She spat a couple of times to clear her mouth of the taste then tried again. "Why them pair? Why are they so special?" she asked him.

"I'm not sure," he said. "It's Hook more than the boy, I think. I just didn't want Hook found yet."

"Does this mean I'm free of you, now?"

"One more job to do, old woman, far away from here and a long time down the road," the man said. "One more and then we're quits and you can die for good."

He passed his hand in front of her face and watched as she faded slowly from view, the chair becoming visible through her body until its broken slats and a blood stain were all that was left to show she had been there.

The man stood, scratching his chin. He smiled at some thought he had then vanished all at once, the air closing in on his space with a clap.

STRANGE LESSONS

Pretty much everyone round these parts knew my Uncle Frank was crazy. His older friends were kinder and used words like 'odd' or 'weird', but to just about everyone else, old Frank was madder than a bag of badgers. There were a lot of things about Uncle Frank that were off centre; for one thing, he had a hankering to wear my Aunt May's under-things beneath his work coverall some days. Christ alone knows why she stuck with him all those years, and I don't think even He's too sure. Frank would do some odd stuff, alright, like the time he took the youngest Wakefield boy round the back of his barn. He had no urge to do anything sexual with the boy – like I say, his only vice along those lines was occasionally wearing old Aunt May's knickers – but he gave the boy his pistol and told him to place it against my Uncle's forehead, right between his eyes.

"Whenever you're ready, son," he said, grinning just as wide as he could. Now the Wakefield boy was only twelve at the time. He took one look at Uncle Frank's eyes and that grin of his, and he damn well pissed himself and took off haring up the street, Uncle Frank's pistol still in his hand.

Another time, Frank gathered his kids to him – he and Aunt May had obviously gotten on well enough as there were three of them – and he lined them up in the garden, all in a row in the potato patch. Those kids knew he wouldn't hurt them as he'd

17

never laid a hand on them without a good reason since they were knee high, and even when he did you could bet your dog that they deserved it. Anyhow, he lined them up and started dancing around them just as fast as you please.

"What you doing Pa?" my cousin Lewis asked. He was the eldest, so he felt it was up to him to try and stop his Pa's foolishness.

"I'm summoning rain, son," Uncle Frank said, still running and dancing and leaping around them. "We ain't had a drop since shit knows when, and if we don't soon then nothing but shit is what we'll have in this potato patch."

Now my cousin Lewis was none too smart himself, him being his daddy's boy and all. Add that to the fact he was about twelve or thirteen at the time and it might make you understand why he reasoned that maybe dancing for rain like some of the Walkers were supposed to do wasn't such a bad idea after all. So, taking his cue from his Pa, he started dancing around the other two kids, my cousins Sarah and Isadora (why Frank gave such a pretty sounding name to a baby that looked like a hog is another thing that's in Christ's know how and no–one else's) and the pair of them, being kids, just up and joined in. Lewis reckoned the four of them danced and ran for close on half an hour, even though they were all out of puff, and he said they'd have probably just carried right on dancing if Aunt May hadn't turned up. She was a wonderful Judas-fearing woman who made the most delicious cookies you ever ate, but she had a temper on her that put anything else in this Land to shame. Lewis said he was more scared of his Ma then than he had been the year before when she'd caught him pulling on his old man and looking at some pictures of naked women his friend had given him. Aunt May dropped her shopping and screamed across the yard at the four of them, stopping them dead in their tracks.

"How many times do I have to tell you, Francis?" she shouted. Like a lot of women, she only ever used her husband's full name when she was pissed at him. "I don't want you teaching the kids none of that . . . that heathen stuff! You kids get inside the house now and out of them clothes!"

All that dancing and jumping around had kicked up dust and dirt and they were fairly covered in it. Lewis said they just ran inside and didn't stop till they were in their room. By this time, Frank's neighbours were all leaning out of their windows, watching my Uncle get the ragging of his life. Aunt May went on for as long as they'd been dancing, Lewis reckoned, and at the end of it he said his Pa had to sleep out in the dog kennel for the night, while all three kids had a hiding dished out by Aunt May and her trusty wooden spoon. Uncle Frank had hardly laid a hand on them since they were kids, like I said, but old Aunt May was a stickler for discipline and whenever she felt they deserved it (which wasn't often as they were good kids on the whole – simple minded, but good) she took to their backsides with the great wooden spoon she used for stirring the stew. It was a day or two later that Lewis told me that story, but he waited till after his Ma was in her grave alongside Uncle Frank before he told me the rest.

"I woke up during the night," he said, "and just felt like I had to look out the window, just to check on my Pa, like, cos he was sleeping in the kennel an' all. Shit me if he weren't up and dancing in the potato patch again, in the middle o' the night, buck naked. I don't know how long he'd been dancing, but his legs were covered in dirt an' all, an' he didn't look like he was gonna stop either.

"I kept watching for another few minutes, feeling like I had to, y'know, an' shit me if it didn't start raining. One minute the night was clear, you could see all the stars and moons, and the next it clouded over and just started belting it down, like Judas Christ himself was taking an almighty piss. An' Pa just carried on dancing in the rain, only now he'd moved over to the patch of grass my Ma called a lawn, an' he started laughing an' laughing like the loon all his so called friends called him behind his back.

"Next morning, Ma didn't say nothing to him, an' he didn't

say nothing to her, but all us kids could see he was happy. He was sure he'd called down the rain, an' Ma wasn't sure enough that he hadn't, if you see what I mean, so she felt like she had to keep quiet."

Now I don't know how much of that story's true, but I do know that during that Season, Uncle Frank had enough potatoes to go round most of his friends and relatives, including my own family.

One other thing he used to do was tell the weather in a manner the like of which I had never seen before and certainly haven't since. Uncle Frank could be just walking down Oxenford's Main Street, which in those days was even less deserving of capital letters than it is now, when he'd just stop dead, looking up at the sky. Around the dry Season in these parts, we get some of the bluest skies I've ever seen, and I've travelled a few places. Frank would just stare up at them, holding his crotch for a few minutes then smart as you please, he'd undo the braces on his coverall and whip them down, showing off Aunt May's drawers to whoever happened to be watching (and more than a few times it was the Mayor and his wife) and then they'd come down too. He'd grab hold of his old man and lift it up, looking at his sack underneath. Seems strange saying this, but he swore blind that when his left ball was hanging down lower than the right, it was time to get your hat and coat and get in anything that would blow away because Frank would tell you a storm was coming.

Most people didn't listen to him at first (Hell, even his own family doubted him) but after they'd lost some washing off the line or some shingles from their roof a few times, they started taking notice of Uncle Frank's balls, if you'll pardon the expression.

Listen to me. I started out on Uncle Frank so I could lead into what I was really going to tell you, but my wife always says that I wouldn't waste a word when a whole page would do.

Uncle Frank was my Pa's eldest brother, so I was related to

him through blood, not just marriage like I was to my Aunt May, and I reckon I've inherited one or two of his traits. Not that I go around looking in my under shorts to check the weather or try to get kids to shoot me, but over the years I figure I've learned to trust one intuition especially and it was this that I really wanted to talk about.

With a town like ours, sat smack across one of the big trade roads into the Mainland Kingdoms, we tend to see a lot of travellers and Strangers coming back and forth. Partly because of that, partly because of the farming land around here, Oxenford's become big enough over the last few years to warrant having a Sheriff and a couple of deputies. Somehow, I landed the job of Sheriff a while back and it seems like I've done a good enough job as I haven't been lynched yet.

A couple of Seasons ago, I was sitting in what is grandly known as the Sheriff's office, but is actually the back room of Edgar's barber shop, doing what I normally do on hot days: I was having a nap, my feet up on my desk, my hat pulled over my head to keep the bright sun that was coming in through the window out of my eyes. There was nothing happening in town that day that needed my attention, so I was taking it pretty easy. My deputies were out keeping an eye on things, Josie in the stables, still trying to get in with the Atkins girl (pretty little thing, with never a bad word to say about anyone) and Mitch was in the Tuppence, the bar on Main Street, slowly getting drunk. Everyone said I should have fired him years before but I liked the kid, even though his head was so full of stories and cheap whisky he could hardly tell what real life was anymore.

As I said, I was having a quiet nap one lunch time when all of a sudden this knack I've got started up in a big way. Normally, I wake up nice and slow, yawning and stretching like any other hard working man, but this day I woke with a snap. One minute I was dreaming of Christ knew what, the next I was sat up straight, reaching for the pistol I kept in my desk drawer. I went out into the barber's a minute or two later, my pistol belt strapped round my waist, the heavy holster laying against my leg. Edgar was near the window, shaving Old Man Howard with that great straight razor he used. Damn thing was almost a foot long, I swear, and no matter how often he offered to shave me for free I still shave myself.

"What's up Sheriff?" Edgar asked as I came out. He noticed my pistol, something I hardly ever needed to wear, and his old eyes widened as much as was possible in that tough, leathery face of his.

"I'm not quite sure, Ed," I replied, walking past the pair and staring out of the window which looked out on to Main Street. There was nobody there that I didn't know, and no–one doing anything wrong, yet my knack had me all fired up as I said.

"Is there going to be trouble?" Edgar asked. Old Man Howard was watching that razor of Ed's as it started shaking near his chin. Ed's a good man and a damn fine barber (even if I won't let him shave me) but he didn't exactly stock up on guts when Christ handed them out.

"You know, Ed," I said quietly, still watching Main Street, "I think there may be."

That was my knack, you see, my intuition, the thing that I'd inherited from Uncle Frank. For some Christ forsaken reason I could always tell when trouble was brewing, though I couldn't always tell where it was coming from. I'd always thought it was a pretty good thing to have, especially being Sheriff, but I've grown to hate it recently. It's pretty hard to live with something that saved my life but couldn't save anyone else's.

"Shit!"

I turned around and wasn't all that surprised to find Edgar had sliced a piece of skin the size of a penny from Old Man Howard's chin in his fright and was frantically trying to stem the flow of blood. I looked back out the window. Trouble was coming, alright.

We get a fair few Strangers in Oxenford. As I said, it's on one of the main roads into the Mainland Kingdoms off to the West and, as there's not that much out to the East between here and the Frontiers, most people travelling on the roads tend to be headed West or down South. A lot of them tend to be Strangers.

They're a curious breed, just like their name implies. Men and women who seemingly just wander around, from Kingdom to Kingdom, doing pretty much what they please for the most part, stopping at towns like ours for a few days then heading off on their way. Most towns that get a few Strangers each Season have a Station reserved for their use, a place where they can stay away from us Natives, get refreshed and eat a good meal. Like any form of hotel, these Stations have a Master who runs the place and who provides for the Strangers that stay there and tries to make sure that peace and quiet are kept.

A few days after my knack woke me up from my afternoon doze, I had a visitor come into the back room of Edgar's shop asking to see me. It was Ben Hallian, the Station Master. I told him to come in and sit down, poured him some of my whisky and offered him a smoke to calm his nerves.

"What's the problem, Ben?" I asked him straight. He looked a bit surprised as he hadn't said anything about any problem, but I didn't need any sort of knack to work out he was worried about something. It was written all over his face, not to mention the way his hands shook as he smoked his jay.

"That knack o'yours, Sheriff. What would you do without it?" he said, looking down at the floor. I saw no point in disillusioning him concerning my knack – it helps if more people believe I've got the damn thing; at least that's what I used to think. I gave him a few minutes to calm himself down and let him get around to things in his own time and, after a few more pulls on his jay and a couple of sips of whisky, he sat back in his chair and looked over at where I sat.

"We got a few new Strangers in the Station, Sheriff."

"How many does that make in total, Ben?"

"The three that came in today make it up to seven now. One of the ones who came in today is a fairly young kid calling himself

23

Justice. He seems to be okay. Looking for a friend of his, another Stranger who he thinks has been through here."

"And has he?"

"No–one recognises the kid's description and there's no record of him in the register, and by the sound of it this other Stranger's fairly distinctive," he paused and took another sip of whisky.

"And the other Strangers that came in today, Ben? What're they like?"

"I think that's where we may have some trouble, Sheriff. One of the other Strangers is a woman."

I looked at Ben with his wide eyes, shaking hands and sweaty brow and couldn't help but feel a little confused. "We've had women Strangers before now, Ben. Not as many as fellas, admittedly, but they ain't that rare."

Ben shook his head as I talked. "I don't mean that we might have trouble because she's a woman, Sheriff. I think we might be in for some trouble because of who she is and who she's with. She's calling herself Ivory and came in with a fella named Rune."

I shrugged, deliberately noncommittal. "Could be another Ivory. Could be another Rune. These Strangers like their fancy, melodramatic names. You of all people should know that, Ben. I mean, we got that young Justice kid who came in today and who else did you say a day or two back? Ain't there a Puritan staying at the Station right now, and a Saxon? Sweet Judas, Ben, you should know better than to get all fired up just because of some Stranger's name."

But again, Ben was just shaking his head the whole time I was talking.

"No, Sheriff. Hate to say it, but you're wrong. I heard her and that Rune fella talking in the bar. Way they was chatting seems they go back a ways, and that Rune seems like a mighty nasty piece of work."

I sighed and finished the last of my whisky, while Ben re–lit his jay with my matches. With finger and thumb of my right

24

hand I rubbed at the bridge of my nose and sighed again.

"This Justice kid. He come in with Ivory and Rune?"

"No, he turned up this morning, round nine. Says he's gonna stay a day or two, get some supplies and move on. Like I said, he's looking for some other Stranger. The other two showed up round dinner."

"What's Ivory look like?"

"Short cropped dark hair, dresses like any other Stranger; kinda normal, but looks a bit odd, you know? Got a leather waistcoat, with britches and boots, and her jacket's ex–army. No badges or insignia, but I'd reckon it was Aymian."

I sighed again. All the Sheriff's offices and Station Masters in and around the Mainland Kingdoms get wanted posters delivered around the start of each Season describing Strangers it might be best to avoid or, if there happens to be a King's Marshall in town at the time, to arrest. One of the worst was this woman Ivory whose trademark, if you like, was her ex–army jacket, supposedly stolen from a Colonel she'd killed during the Cynian–Aymian wars ten years back. Strangers have a penchant for things that make them stand out, be it their names or the style of clothes they wore.

"They say how long they were staying?" I asked him.

"No, just that they were waiting for somebody to turn up."

"Was this just any old someone or are they waiting for a specific person?"

Ben shook his head. "Didn't say, Sheriff. Ivory said she'd wait until someone showed up. To be honest, I don't think she's really waiting for anyone; she's just using that as some sort of excuse to hang around."

"Okay. Marshall McKinley ain't due for –" I flipped through some papers till I found the one I wanted and read it. "– for another Season or so, so he ain't no help," I sighed and looked over at him. "You go on back to the Station, Ben. Anything untoward happens, you ring the bell and me, Josie and Mitch'll be right there."

25

"Christ, Sheriff, you know as well as I do Mitch wouldn't be any use against a Stranger like this Ivory. Hell, I doubt he's much use against a Native."

"Go on back to the Station, Ben. Any fuss, ring the bell. If there's no trouble before, I'll be over with Josie and Mitch later this evening to have a little chat with our new arrivals. Go on, now. Get."

Ben left my office no happier than he was when he came in. I don't know whether or not he had expected me to rush into the Station and start shooting the place up just because he had a couple of bad Strangers in there, but any attempt I'd made to ease his mind didn't seem to have worked. Truth be told, my own mind wasn't that eased. Most Strangers were like this Justice kid Ben had mentioned: they go about their own business, just passing through our towns. But it seemed like for every couple of "normal" Strangers, you had one who was rotten to the core, Strangers like this Ivory and her friend Rune who more than made up for the amount of trouble you could expect from any other Stranger.

I dug out the posters I kept in my desk drawer. The Sheriff before me used to pin copies of them up around the town, but I stopped that when I got the job. Townsfolk used to see them posters, get up a lynching mob and make for some of the Strangers that came through. Didn't matter to them that some of the people they hanged turned out to be innocent.

I had posters on both Ivory and Rune. Both were murderers. They'd served as mercenaries during the Cynian–Aymian wars and had seen more than their fair share of action. Somewhere along the line, though, they'd overstepped the mark and turned into killers. Rumour had it that they'd gone West out to the Funeral Wastes beyond the Kingdoms, and whatever they had seen or done out there had changed them. They had no regard for human life anymore. They didn't care.

One of the worst things about being a town Sheriff is that you have very little jurisdiction over Strangers. Some useless, age–old law states only a King's Marshall can arrest a Stranger; a lowly Sheriff can only report them. Or shoot them. There were only a few times I really regretted having this job. This looked like one of them.

Like I'd told Ben, later that evening Josie, Mitch and me went over to the Station, looking to have a chat with Ivory and Rune. I'd told Josie and Mitch to wear their pistols tonight; not too obviously, I didn't want to start trouble in my own town, but just to make sure the Strangers knew we were armed. Neither of the boys were much good with the damn things anyway, but I figured every little helped, and if wearing some shooting irons helped them to get their wind up for when they confronted these Strangers, then I wasn't about to stop them.

When we arrived at the Station, however, we found that both Ivory and Rune had gone.

"Gone where, Ben? To bed? To the bar? Out of town?"

"They've gone over to the Tuppence, Sheriff."

For a man whose job was dealing with Strangers day in and day out, Ben was definitely shook up over this pair and I thought maybe I should start being a little more concerned than I had been.

"Okay, Ben," I said a little gentler. "Did they say when they'd be back?" He shook his head. "Then me and the boys here will take a stroll over to the Tuppence and have a chat with Ivory and her friend."

"Ain't you gonna leave Mitch here, Sheriff?" The way he said it didn't sound like he was asking for protection, rather it seemed the only way he could think of to say he didn't consider Mitch was worth anything against these Strangers.

"Aye cun look ayfter ma'sayulf, Mistah Hally–yan," Mitch said in that slow, crawling, Christ–awful accent of his. Even now I still don't know why I ever took on anyone who talked like that. He claimed he'd come up North from the Blue States, though I'll be damned if I ever heard anyone else from there talk like that.

Ben looked him up and down, noted the pistol against his thigh and laughed in his face. "Don't know what you're doing with him as a deputy, Sheriff. Man's a dullard and a drunk."

"Thank you for that, Ben. But whether you like it or not, Mitch here is my deputy and he's coming over to the Tuppence with me to go and chat to the Strangers you've said are possible trouble makers. Keep your lights on. We may be back soon," I tipped my hat at him and left, Mitch and Josie following me. It's only a minute or two's walk to the Tuppence from the Station and as much as I would have liked to stop and ask Mitch just what Ben Hallian's problem was with him, I figured there was a job to be done first.

The bar of the Tuppence was pretty much like any other bar you can find on the outskirts of the Mainland Kingdoms. Two swing doors led straight into the main room with the bar directly opposite you, but nowhere else had pretty Sarah Woodrow stood behind it, pouring out beers and whisky for the few customers. Round tables, each with about three or four chairs around them, ran the length of each wall forming a sort of aisle from the doors up to the bar, which in turn had high stools along it. A few people saw me and the boys come in and shouted hellos, though there were a few confused looks when they saw our pistols. Despite what Ben had said, by the time I'd walked up to the bar and said hi to Sarah, I still hadn't seen anyone fitting the description of Ivory.

"Sheriff. Boys. What can I get you?" Sarah asked as she wiped the top of the bar down with a cloth. Mitch started to ask for a whisky from force of habit, but I over rode him and said "One whisky and two beers, please Sarah," As she went off to pour them I looked around the bar again, this time trying to put names to the faces of the Strangers I could see.

Sat at a table farthest away from the bar, his legs stretched out in front of him, a hooded cloak over his shoulders and a beer in his hands was the Stranger I'd met a day or two previous, named

28

Saxon. Every time Ben had a new Stranger in the Station who was intending to stay more than a couple of nights, I made a point of going over there and making myself known. Never does any harm, and it lets the Strangers know that there's someone in town who's keeping a friendly eye on them.

On the table next to him, hunched over a book no less, was a young kid, in his early twenties at the most, with his black hair spiked up from wearing his hat, and a feathered braid running down the length of it from behind his ear. Must be Justice, I figured, the young Stranger that had come in at nine that morning. I hadn't had a chance to meet him yet, but planned on strolling over and saying howdy in a moment or two.

The table next to him held Old Man Howard and his poker cronies, guys like Daniel Coomes, one of the most mean spirited men it has ever been my misfortune to know, and his brother Simon who, not surprisingly, was just about the second most mean spirited son of a bitch I'd ever met. Playing fourth with them was the Reverend Teague, and the less said about him the better.

The only other Stranger in the bar was sat on his own on the next table, though I noticed there were two full beer glasses on the table. He was a tall guy even sat down, and wore a long brown leather overcoat, dirt and road dust caked into the creases of the arms and shoulders. His hat sat on the table next to his beer, wide brimmed but not very tall. Being the size he was I dare say he didn't need to worry about how much extra his hat added to his height.

"There you go Sheriff," Sarah said bringing our drinks over. I gave her a couple of crowns and picked up my whisky.

"Stay here, fellas. I'm gonna go over and say howdy to our new boys in town," Just before I moved off, I looked at Mitch and, in a lower voice, said "Stay clear of the whisky, Mitch. I might need you straight tonight, and I don't want to give Hallian any more reason to dislike you than he already has." He nodded and sipped gently at his beer. I walked down the length of the bar, smiling to a couple of the other guys I knew in there, nodding politely to Old Man Howard but ignoring his buddies, who in turn ignored me, and stopped at Justice's table.

"Mind if I sit with you, Stranger?" I asked him.

He looked up at me, noting my pistol first and my badge second and held out his hand, indicating the other seat at the table. "Sure, Sheriff."

"You're Justice, right?" I sat opposite him, watching as he placed a scrap of paper in the book to mark his place and put it on the table. I glanced at the brown paper cover which had *Strayngers: Men or Miths?* in big bold letters at the top and the author's name, Rev R. J. Diver beneath it.

"Good book?" I asked him. He smiled and looked down at the book, taking a gulp from his beer before answering.

"No, I can't say it is. It's perhaps the worst thing I've ever read concerning us folks."

"Can't say as I've ever read anything along those lines myself. What makes it so bad?"

He looked over at me and leaned forward intently. "The dear Reverend Ronald John Diver here," he tapped the book's cover, "seems unable to decide whether or not Strangers actually exist as a kind of separate class of people, or whether it's just an instinctive dislike the Natives have of anyone or anything different that singles them out. And he will swear until he's red in the face that there is no way that the good lord Judas Christ was a Stranger, but that the man who was hung from a tree in that potter's field all those years ago was a Native through and through."

I stared back at him for a second or two before clearing my throat.

"Sounds like a hefty kinda book," I said. "Not sure I'd understand it if I tried to read it."

"An honest Sheriff?" he said, laughing. "I'm sorry, I didn't mean to make fun of you." He picked up the book again and looked at it. "It is hard reading, but that doesn't necessarily make

30

it any better than those pulps you can pick up at the hardware store for a couple of pennies. Fact is Sheriff, the Reverend R. J. Diver goes so far out of his way to come over as intelligent and learned that he ends up talking a load of horse shit. Sometimes the cheapest piece of pulp trash can contain far more worth than any half-assed intellectual pamphlet produced by some religious bigot, and some of the most important lessons can be found in the most unlikely places. Even places like this, Sheriff."

"Seems like you and religion don't get on to well, Stranger."

He smiled again and leaned back in his chair.

"It's not like that, Sheriff. I kinda like the religion, but I don't really like its preachers. Whether it's Judas Christ, the Cuckoo God, R'lyeh or some other god they're talking about, they're all convinced their way is right. Trouble is, some of them have to be wrong."

I smiled back at him and nodded towards the poker players on the next table. They hadn't seemed to hear anything; not because they were so wrapped up in their game but because all the old bastards were practically deaf as posts. "Maybe you'd better not say that too loud around old Reverend Teague there. He may be a cantankerous son of a bitch, but he's got enough believers in this town to cause you some trouble."

"I ain't out to cause trouble, Sheriff. Like I told the Station Master, I'm looking for another Stranger, name of Hook, and, seeing as how he ain't been through here, I'll probably be moving on tomorrow."

"Sounds fair enough," I leaned back in my chair and looked past the poker crew up towards Rune, who was still sat on his own. Looking back at Justice, I asked him whether he knew anything about the other Stranger.

"Rune? I've heard of him, but hadn't seen him till today. He's apparently a bit of a hard case, a tough man," he sighed and took a drink of his beer. "Strangers don't normally kill each other unless there's some sort of feud between them. We pretty much either stick together or just ignore each other. What we don't do

31

is kill each other for the hell of it; there's few enough of us as it is." He leaned forward again, his elbows on the table, his voice quieter. "I've seen four dead Strangers, all apparently killed by Rune for no reason at all. Now I don't know whether he did kill them, but it wouldn't surprise me if he had. You've got a bad Stranger in town, Sheriff."

"The Station Master says I might have two."

"How so?"

"Rune came into town with another Stranger calling herself Ivory. Name mean anything to you?"

Justice looked down at the table and scratched at the stubble on his cheek. "I've met two Ivory's in my time, Sheriff. One was an absolute peach of a girl that I almost fell in love with a year or so ago," he looked up at me with all the good humour gone from his eyes. "The other was the meanest bitch I ever met. If you have got that Ivory in town, Sheriff, I wouldn't bother waiting for her to start anything. I wouldn't bother trying to find a Marshall. Shoot her as soon as you see her, because that's what she's probably going to do to you. No bad mouthing each other. No big build up. No threats. If she gets the idea in her head to shoot you, she will, and she won't lose any sleep over it." He picked up his book, stuffed it into the pocket of his jacket and stood up. "I'm gonna get back to the Station and pack my stuff. Seems like I might make an earlier start than I planned. Take care, Sheriff."

I watched him as he walked out of the bar, nodding to Saxon on the way, then I picked up my beer, which I'd hardly touched, and stood up myself. I looked over at Josie and Mitch who were still stood at the bar, the pair of them trying their damnedest to look relaxed, neither of them doing such a good job. I smiled at them, in the hope of relieving their worries or something, but it didn't seem to have any effect. Taking a deep breath, steadying my nerves and trying not to think about what Justice had said, I walked past Old Man Howard and his poker buddies and stood next to Rune's table.

"Howdy, Stranger," I said. "Mind if I sit down?"

He tilted his head back and looked at me with narrow eyes, almost as if he were squinting against the sun. He casually looked me up and down, noting my badge and pistol just as Justice had done a few minutes earlier, but in a much colder manner, reminding me of how Turner the butcher sizes up a cow at market.

"Free country," he said, returning his gaze to his beer.

I sat down opposite him, wondering how to open a conversation. Seems odd to think back on it now, but everything I'd heard about both Rune and Ivory that night, first from Ben Hallian then from Justice, had unsettled me, shook me up. I glanced over at my deputies, grimacing as I saw Mitch carefully nursing a whisky while Josie was leaning over the bar, getting as close as possible to Sarah the barmaid. The table where Saxon had sat was now empty as well. When I turned back to Rune, he was staring at me, unblinking.

"You're —" I started, then coughed, clearing my throat. "You're Rune, right?" I said. The tall Stranger just stared at me. I tried smiling, to almost make a joke of what I said next. "Heard some bad things about you. Hope you're not planning on any trouble?" I'd hoped to make it light, to make him aware that while I didn't want any trouble, I could handle any that he dished out. At the time I didn't quite believe myself, and I know damn well he didn't.

"Do you want some trouble?" he asked quietly, still staring at me.

"That's just what I don't want," I replied as quickly as possible. Perhaps too quickly, thinking back on it. "Just thought I'd, y'know, come over and introduce myself. Say howdy and have a talk."

"Your momma never tell you not to talk to Strangers?" He reached into his coat pocket and brought out some matches, rolling papers and tobacco, but no grass. As I watched, and with his eyes still on me, never once looking at his fingers, he rolled a straight, one-handed, placed it between his lips and popped a match alight with his thumbnail, lighting up his smoke and drawing deep on it.

"First time in a crow's age I seen someone smoke a straight," I said with a smile, still trying to be friendly.

"I don't hold with drugs. Mess up your mind."

"Matter of opinion I suppose. Myself, why I quite enjoy –"

"What do you want?" It was said quietly with no real force behind it, but that sentence cut me dead. Unless it was my imagination, just about everyone at the bar seemed to shut up instantly, even the deaf poker players, everybody looking at our table.

I don't mind admitting it now, after it's all been and gone, and after what happened, but I was scared then. This Rune scared me, the way he appeared not to have a care in the Land, the way he could be so quiet and yet command such presence, the way he never blinked. I don't know how I did it, but I leaned across the table and stared at him. I could feel the sweat under my arms dirtying my shirt and more starting to run down my back and the thing I wanted to do most at that instant was just bail out, head back to my office behind Ed's barber shop and sit with some whisky and a few jays.

"I want you to know that your kind ain't welcome in this town," I said quietly, hoping to Judas that my voice sounded as steady to him as it did to me. "We don't want bad Strangers here, Rune. Maybe you'd better leave before someone gets hurt. Nobody here wants any –"

"This little fuck bothering you, Rune?"

The voice came from behind me, soft and feminine, marred only by the obscenity she spoke. It didn't take an expert to work out who stood behind me. An arm, in the sleeve of an ex–army jacket, reached forward and picked up the beer that had stood with Rune's.

"No, Ive. He ain't bothering me," Rune still stared, and for the first time the sides of his mouth curled up in the smallest example of a smug, self–satisfied smile that I've ever seen. "Actual fact, he was just asking me to leave."

There was the sound of smacking wet lips and a gasp, before the beer glass was returned to the table, empty. "Yeah? What the fuck you been up to then?"

"Well, to tell you the truth, Ive, I don't know. The good Sheriff here just wants me out of town for no reason."

Now it wasn't my imagination. Everyone in the bar was quiet. Nobody said a word, there was no clink of glasses, no laughter, nothing. Unless my intuition was all shot to hell, everyone was looking at the three of us, and I prayed to Christ that that included my two deputies. I felt a small hand fall lightly on my shoulder.

"If he ain't done fuck all, how come you want his scrawny ass out of this shit hole of a town?" Ivory asked me. "Seems a little unfuckingfair to me."

That was when I had another flash from that knack that I inherited from Uncle Frank. Trouble was, I wasn't quick enough this time. Since it happened, I've tried kidding myself it was because Ivory was just too quick and that there was nothing I could have done anyway, but I think now, with hindsight, the reason I didn't speak up was because I was scared, more scared than I ever had been before and certainly since. What I wanted to say, to shout, was "No, Mitch, don't!" but I was too damned scared.

I turned my head, knowing what I was going to see. Mitch stood, fumbling for his pistol as he yelled "That's enough!" I tried to call out to him, to stop him, but Ivory was way ahead of me, her pistol in her hand firing off three shots before Mitch had his gun out of his holster. Each shot caught him in the chest, blowing chunks of him out of his back, leaving gaping holes in his body, propelling him backwards, the last shot pushing him on top of the bar, his arms splayed out, blood pooling beneath him and dripping from the surface of the bar. Sarah the barmaid screamed and dropped a couple of bottles she was holding, the sound of the smashing glass a strange counterpoint to the blasts from Ivory's pistol.

"Shut up, bitch," Ivory said and shot her in the head, her pretty blonde hair mixed with brains spraying over the mirror behind the bar before she dropped to the floor and lay amongst the blood and broken bottles.

Two men, I found out later it was the Reverend's son and his friend Mark, stood up, obviously going for their own guns, but Rune stood up, all seven feet of him, a shiny silver pistol in each hand, the like of which I'd never seen before, and let off three shots from each, blasting the two men against the wall, leaving their lives splashed on the wood in bright red stains.

"Chris!" the Reverend shouted, standing up and beginning to move towards his son. I never liked him, but I'd rather he was still alive all the same. As soon as he moved, Rune just pointed one of his guns at him, not even deigning to look at him, and shot him in the neck, the force of the bullet spinning him around and on to the floor, leaving him with blood jetting almost up to the ceiling, before it diminished, painting the wall with weaker spurts as he died.

"Oh shit," Josie cried as he reached, finally, for his own gun, but again the Strangers were just too quick. The pair of them turned and shot him together, arranging him almost perfectly against Mitch on the bar. He coughed once, sending a fine spray of blood into the air, then died.

"Well shit, Sheriff, now it looks like we've fucking done something for you to want us out of this fucked up town!" Ivory said with a laugh.

"No more killing. Please," I said, scared out of my wits. Six people, two of them my own deputies, had been shot in the space of about twenty seconds. Six lives ended instantly with the pulling of a trigger. Six human beings who would never breathe, eat, love, hate or do anything ever again. "No more killing. Please," I repeated, feeling tears begin to well up in my eyes.

"Don't cry, Sheriff," Ivory said walking around to stand next to Rune so that I could see her face for the first time. Even through my tears she was beautiful, her short dark hair laying close on her skull, her skin faultless, eyes that would not have looked out of place in an angel's face. Casually, she replaced the six bullets she'd used to kill Mitch, Sarah and Josie, then looked back at me, an impish smile on her lovely lips. "You didn't think we'd forget you, did you?" she asked raising her pistol.

"Why?" I asked, the basic question every child asks when confronted with anything he doesn't understand. What made her do these things, as Justice had said, with no big build up and no threats? How could she kill without thinking?

"Why do you do this?" I asked weakly.

"Who knows?" she answered, and shot me in the chest.

As they left the bar, they shot six other people, including Old Man Howard and his poker buddies. They returned to the Station and shot Ben Hallian, although he managed to survive. Then they rode off, shooting and killing two young lovers who had gone out for stroll beneath the moons. Both Justice and Saxon had returned to the Station, packed their gear and left, according to Hallian. The other Strangers staying there were lucky enough to be out.

I survived Ivory's gunshot, though only just. As she walked around the table to stand next to Rune, I had another flash of that knack I've got and as she raised her pistol at me, I leaned back in the chair. Just before she fired, I pushed back with my feet, toppling the chair backwards and the bullet that would have gone through my heart instead went below it. I still would have died, though, if one of the people they hadn't shot hadn't been the local sawbones, Doc Friday. The man used to be a terrible doctor, constantly on the booze, but since that evening he's never been in a bar since. I'm just glad he wasn't too far gone to sort me out as I lay bleeding on the floor.

Ivory's and Rune's crimes were sent off to the Halls of Justice in Jerusalem and at the start of each Season I get a poster on them both, with the killings of twelve of my town's folks and two deputies just slotted in with the rest of their crimes, as if fourteen lives are just another statistic to the people who run this damned Land.

I almost gave up the post of Sheriff after that, and Ben Hallian did give up control of the Station, but I carried on. I'm wary of every Stranger we get in nowadays and if they cause me any trouble . . . well, I shoot them. I try not to kill anyone, although I have killed a couple, but that night in the Tuppence taught me that being a nice jovial Sheriff doesn't always work. It's not a lesson I enjoyed learning, and not for a second do I think I've become a better man for it, but I do what I have to now, and I refuse to let anyone, Stranger or Native, tell me otherwise.

A good example was the Stranger Justice was looking for, name of Hook. He passed through a week or so afterwards and, even though I was still in bandages, I hounded him out of town. Damn ugly man with a heart to match, and I've often hoped that he and Justice met up somewhere along the road so that Justice could get that bastard off his back and on with his life.

I often think back on the brief conversation I had with Justice, him talking about important lessons being found in unlikely places and I wonder whether we have unwittingly shared a similar experience, whether he's gone through the same sort of thing that I did that night, and I think that it's likely. My wife complains that since that night I've almost become a Stranger myself and who knows, if I was Justice's age, maybe I would have taken on some Strange name and walked out of town.

Who knows?

THE UNDERTAKER'S MESSAGE

Old Thomas the undertaker stood in front of the horse drawn hearse, hands clasped behind his back. His long, black tail coat flapped in the chill wind that charged down the hill, seeming to dodge between the gravestones, carrying with it snowflakes like some out of place confetti. Behind him stood his assistants, Blake and Jennings, both young men only just out of the Elder Tree and acting as attendants at the funeral. In front of them, a little way further down the hill, the actual funeral was nearing its end, the body being lowered into the six feet deep hole by means of a rope around its neck. The rope was attached to a pulley at the top of a tall gantry erected over the grave. The shroud in which the body was wrapped rippled and snapped in the wind.

"Tis a cold day for a burial, sir," Jennings said rubbing his hands together to try and warm them.

"Hold your tongue and your hands still, boy. The mourners do not wish to see your pitiful attempts to encourage warmer blood."

Jennings placed his hands behind his back, his head bowed, frantically trying to stop hopping from one foot to another to keep warm. The two mourners, a middle aged woman and an older man, separated by some thirty years, held each other around the shoulders, shaking and shivering with a combination of grief and cold. The woman raised her hand and wiped a few tears from her cheeks before they could freeze over and remain as fragile trails across her skin.

" . . . and so it is, we put Matthew in the ground, lowering him by a rope in the same way that our Lord Judas was let down from his own noose all those years ago. Amen."

The Sermoner stood with his own hands thrust deep in the pockets of his breeches, a scarf wrapped around his neck, a copy of the Book tucked under his arm and an expression of boredom mixed with a desire to be before a warm fire clearly stamped on his face. He walked around the grave in which the body stood vertically, a set of rods and ties running along the length of the corpse to prevent it collapsing upon itself. With the woman on one side and he on the other, the Sermoner guided the old man away from the grave, allowing the two sextons, who had stood nearby, to come forward and begin filling the grave.

"Notice how the Sermoner and sextons all wish to be inside and warm," Old Thomas said over his shoulder to Blake and Jennings. "The funeral service was rushed and poorly read. The Sermoner himself is merely the Reverend's understudy. Nothing is sacred any longer, boys, not even death." He glanced briefly at his two assistants and sighed gently. "The weather affects you both also, if I am not mistaken, and you too wish to be inside and warm. The Elder Tree is not producing such fine fruit as once it did."

With a gesture from their master, Blake and Jennings climbed aboard the covered wagon that served as a hearse while Old Thomas untied his own horse from a nearby tree and mounted it. At a steady pace, he lead the two young men driving the wagon down towards the town of White Stone. As they left the graveyard, the wind eased for a moment, and snow began to fall steadily.

"I would like to visit the Reverend later this evening."

Holland looked up at the undertaker as he stood before his desk, his hands characteristically clasped behind his back. He had known the visiting undertaker from the Frontiers for several years, and in all that time he doubted that he had ever seen the grim old man smile even once.

"Any particular reason, Thomas?"

"The funeral today of Matthew, son of Joseph. The Sermoner who read at the internment was more preoccupied with the warmth of his body than the reading from the Book. Indeed, for the latter part of the reading, the Book was clasped between his arm and his ribs. His hands were in his pockets."

Holland dropped the pencil he had been holding on to his desk and leaned back in his chair.

"That at least is understandable, Thomas. We're having the coldest Season for years. Some of the older folks say it's the coldest ever. No one really wants to stand for half an hour beside the grave of some dead bum and mumble words that mean nothing to the mourners."

Old Thomas stood before Holland's desk and stared at him until he began to fidget.

"With utterances such as those, Mr. Holland, White Stone is in danger of becoming a heathen place."

"Hell, Thomas. There are more faiths than just Judas, you know that. A lot of people don't want a Judan burial for their relatives or themselves. Only last week I had to arrange for a member of the Church of the Cuckoo God to officiate at a funeral."

"Other faiths, Mr. Holland? There are no other faiths. Judas Christ was hung from a tree by his neck eighteen hundred years ago for –"

"Exactly, Thomas!" Holland stood up behind his desk and planted both hands on the top, glaring at the old man before him. "Exactly. Eighteen hundred years is a Hell of a long time. Not everyone round here cares too much for Judas and his bunch of friends and the further West you go, the fewer followers he has. Now I don't know what it's like back in the Frontier towns like Kingston –"

41

"We are all Judan there and proud of it."

"Yeah, you don't surprise me too much with that. But this is one of the Mainland Kingdoms, Thomas. Things work differently here. No one really cares too much if some drunk gets shot by a Stranger in town. Hell, from what I hear only Matthew's wife and Pa showed up anyhow, and both of them ain't got the sense they were born with. You didn't know Matthew like we did. The man was a menace. Way most people figure it, this Hook guy's done White Stone a favour."

"Hook?" Old Thomas asked.

"Yeah. Some Stranger who walked into town a day or two back. The Sheriff's had a word with him about things and it seems Matthew drew a gun first. Witnesses back up the Stranger's story," Holland narrowed his eyes and stared at the undertaker. "You okay there, Thomas?" he asked.

"Fine," he said, his voice wavering slightly. Normally pallid, the old man's weather worn face had drained of all colour except for two hectic spots of red riding high on his cheeks. "What does . . . this Hook . . . look like?"

"Hell, Thomas, sit down before you fall down, man," Holland came out from behind his desk and took his arm.

"What does Hook look like?" Old Thomas asked through gritted teeth.

"Never mind the Stranger, Thomas —" Holland began to move him towards one of the guest chairs near the fire.

"Get off me!" the undertaker cried, shrugging off Holland's arm. He reached for his hat from the stand and jammed it tight upon his head. "Is he still in town?"

"Who?"

"Hook, you fool!"

"Uh, yeah, I guess. Listen, Thomas —" Before Holland could finish, Old Thomas was out of the door.

It had been many years since Old Thomas had entered a bar. Such a large part of the ordinary people's lives seemed to revolve around the places, particularly in the Frontier towns, but he had given that up many years before, far more than he cared to remember if the truth had to be told. Since graduating from the Elder Tree University, he had touched alcohol on only three occasions, but he had never entered a bar. As a consequence, he stood across the street from the bar, trying to find the courage to enter and confront Hook.

He had already travelled to the Station in search of him, but the Master there had said Hook had left for the bar. In response to Thomas's question of which bar, the Station Master had merely laughed and said that all the Strangers who came to White Stone only went to one bar: Babylon's Gates.

Old Thomas briskly rubbed his hands together, seeming to feel the cold for the first time since his arrival here that morning. He had been at a neighbouring town to officiate over the burial of the Mayor – who had apparently died while making love to his young and energetic wife – and when that funeral was over, he had been called to perform the same rites here for a drunkard shot dead by a Stranger. Had he been inclined, Old Thomas may have laughed at how his profession spanned all classes. Shrugging his shoulders, the undertaker stepped out into the street and crossed over to Babylon's Gates, dodging the slight traffic of horses and carts.

"What can I get you, friend?" the barman asked him as he reached the bar. Old Thomas stood for a moment, dazzled by the lights reflected from glasses, mirrors and polished tankards, the pools of candlelight tanned brown as they shone through whisky bottles, refracting in each one.

"Do you want something or are you just gonna look at the pretty lights?"

"I . . . I'm sorry?" Thomas replied, blinking away his confusion.

The barman threw the cloth he had over his shoulder down on to the bar. "Listen, friend, if you want a beer say so, if not the door's behind you."

"Ah, yes. Sorry. Ah, soda, please," the undertaker managed.

The Stranger stood next to him at the bar snickered and looked down at the floor. The barman sighed heavily, poured a tall glass of soda from a bottle and thumped it on to the bar in front of Old Thomas. As the barman took his money to the till and then returned with his change, Thomas asked him if he knew of a Stranger named Hook.

"I just work here. You wanna ask about someone in particular, ask the owner over there in the corner." He pointed to the end of the bar where two men sat talking in a cubicle, separated from the rest of the room by a thin partition on one side.

"Which one is the owner?"

"John Skin-Dancer, the one with the eye patch," the barman said, turning to serve someone else. Taking a large gulp of his soda, Old Thomas walked over to the cubicle, glancing around the room as he did. Some of the dozen or so tables were empty, though most held some Strangers, mostly men but some women, who sat around talking with each other, drinking beer or whisky. As he approached the cubicle, the two men's conversation became clear.

"R'lyeh no longer sleeps, John; he is awake and calling to his followers. I've heard him," the man opposite John was hooded, his face mostly hidden.

"So what's going to happen, Saxon? Big ball of fire? Huge flood? Death of the first born?" John said with a chuckle.

"Too Judan," Saxon said, his voice holding no humour. "The Ruiner comes, the Land will end. The Cuckoo God cares not, Judas Christ is dead, the Land Lord has left, only R'lyeh stands against him. He will choose someone to strike against the Laughing Man, someone he will not expect," he stood up, pushing his hood back a little. "I am not good with people, John, but you have been a friend. It saddens me that I will not see you again."

He reached across the table and shook Skin-Dancer's hand.

"Well, you never know what happens in this Land of ours.

We might all make it through the end of the world. If you bump into Dale anytime soon, tell him to call in."

Saxon nodded then stepped out of the booth and walked out of the bar. Skin-Dancer watched him go, a frown on his face.

Old Thomas walked forward and coughed politely to attract the owner's attention. He felt entirely out of place, surrounded by Strangers in a bar in a town he did not know. The owner looked up at him with his right eye, the left covered by a patch of black leather.

"Excuse me. Ah, are you the owner?"

"That depends."

"Ah. Um, upon what?"

"If you owe me money then I am, if I owe you then I'm not," the man smiled at his own joke. "Name's John Skin-Dancer. What can I do for you, friend?"

"I'm ah . . . I'd like to . . . to talk with a Stranger here. Hook. His name's Hook."

Skin-Dancer leaned back in his chair and looked up at the old man before him. He rolled a jay, sprinkling ready mixed leaf into the papers. "Now why would you want to talk with him?" he asked, putting the jay in his mouth and lighting it.

"I'd just like to . . . to talk with him."

"Friend, you ain't from the Sheriff's office, you ain't from the Station and you ain't from the brothel. Now they're the people who generally want talk to one of the Strangers here. We don't get many freelancers like you in here, so I get curious when somebody who looks to be an undertaker turns up. I find myself asking why you would want to talk with Hook?"

Old Thomas swallowed a couple of times, then carefully placed his glass of soda on the table before him.

"I'm sorry. I seem to have wasted your time. Sorry," he turned and started away but stopped dead when Skin-Dancer called out to the whole bar:

"Anyone know where Hook is? This gent wants to talk with him."

45

Everyone in the bar, including the barman, turned and stared at Old Thomas as he stood frozen to the spot. Eventually a Stranger sat at a table with two others said,

"Yeah, he's upstairs with Mrs. Karnstein."

"There you go, friend. Why don't you take a seat and Hook'll be down shortly, after he's finished with Mrs. Karnstein," Old Thomas turned around and looked at Skin-Dancer's smiling face. He picked up his soda, headed for the table furthest away and sat down on his own.

"What can I do for you, undertaker?"

Old Thomas watched as the Stranger placed a large rucksack on the floor and sat opposite him, folding up his tall, sparse frame into the chair across the table, appearing to be made up of knees and elbows. His drawn and lined face was marked across the top lip by a network of white scars, insufficiently hidden by the scrub of beard and moustache he wore. His hair rose from the top of his head in wild spikes and tumbled past his shoulders and had turned completely white since Thomas had last set eyes on him.

"It is you."

Hook smiled, leaned back in his chair and put his feet up on the table.

"Yeah, it's me. Who the Hell are you?" He reached into his waistcoat pocket and pulled out a ready rolled jay, lighting it with a match from another pocket.

"A few years ago," Old Thomas stopped and tried to clear his throat. Now that he was sat here, Hook opposite him, he found he was unsure what to say, and doubted the wisdom of his coming. "Do you remember a town called Kingston?"

Hook grinned around his jay. "That's way out East in the Frontiers ain't it?" Old Thomas nodded. "Yeah, I remember the place. Had my ass kicked there a few years back. Ain't likely to forget that. What's it to you, anyway? Larry!" He suddenly shouted across to the barman. "Get me a beer, will ya? And

46

whatever the undertaker here's drinking."

"Do you remember Tom Dunn?"

Hook stared off into space for a second or two taking a drag on his jay and blowing the smoke out of his nose. He shook his head. "Can't say I do."

"You beat him up. In the bar in Kingston. Said you'd . . . raped his wife. He died a week after you left."

The barman arrived with a glass of beer for Hook and another soda for Old Thomas. The undertaker watched Hook take a large gulp of his pint, smacking his lips in satisfaction as he put the glass down.

Hook stared at Thomas, and puffed on his jay. "So?"

"So?" Old Thomas repeated. "You killed a man. You destroyed his life, first mentally then physically. I had to bury one of my neighbours, someone I had known for years, and all you can say is so?"

"Undertaker," he swung his legs off the table and leaned forward. "I shot some guy four days ago because he mouthed off to me. Ain't the first, chances are it won't be the last. Killing people ain't that worrying to me any more," he leaned back and smiled. "Besides, you got the trade didn't you?"

"How can —"

"What do you want me to say, old man? That was what? Five years ago? I don't even remember what the guy looked like. Hell, I can't even remember his wife and Christ knows I should have a better chance with her." He leaned forward again, his hands spread wide. "I can't say I'm sorry, because I'm not. I can't say I'm never gonna do it again, because I almost certainly will. What do you want from me, undertaker?"

Old Thomas looked down at his drink.

"I don't know. I . . . I heard you were in town. I had to see. See whether it was you."

"Far as I know, no other Stranger's called Hook," he smiled again, resuming his position of feet on the table, leaning back in the chair. "Though there is maybe one other Stranger you should know about."

Old Thomas lifted his eyes to Hook's gaze, his hands clasped on the table, his eyebrows raised.

"There's a Stranger been looking for me since round about the time of my . . . indiscretion in Kingston. His name's Justice. I was following him up until a while back, but somehow he's managed to get behind me again. Should be passing through here in about three days if my reckoning is right. Mean son of a bitch, undertaker, real nasty piece of work," Hook smiled as he took another drag on his jay, followed by his beer. Old Thomas stared at him.

"It's Jimmy, isn't it? Jimmy Hayfield?"

Hook laughed loudly, causing some of the other Strangers in the bar to turn and look at them.

"Well, I'd kinda forgotten his real name, but yeah, it's Jimmy, though he calls himself Justice these days. He's been on my ass ever since I left Kingston that night."

It was Old Thomas's turn to smile at the Stranger. "He swore he'd find you."

"Yeah, well, he ain't done it yet. And, to tell you the truth, undertaker, I'm getting mighty tired of him being on my tail and all, so I'd like you to do me a favour," he looked over at the old man in black, reaching forward to stub out his jay on the surface of the table. "I told him some stuff that night in Kingston, mostly to just play with his head, pay him back for kicking my ass. Didn't expect the kid to take it to heart so much, if I'm honest. Still, he has and, like I said, he's been following me ever since and I've had just about enough of it.

"I want you to pass on a message to him. Tell him if he wants me, I'll be up North, probably in the town of Anchorhead. Tell him to find the Ivory Gang. We'll be around there somewhere."

"If you're that tired of things, why not wait here and meet him?"

Hook stood up and drained the last of his beer.

"I may be tired, undertaker, but I'm not an idiot. I want to live free and do my own thing again. I'm sick of being the bad man in his stupid little quest, but I'm not sick of living. If he wants me bad enough, that's where I'll be. And so will my friends," he winked at the old man, picked up his rucksack and walked towards the door.

"Hey, Hook!" Both Hook and Old Thomas turned towards the speaker, the one eyed owner of the pub. "You ain't paid your tab!"

"That's okay, John. The undertaker's paying," and with that, he walked out of the door.

Blake and Jennings, Old Thomas's assistants from the University of The Elder Tree, the training school for undertakers, waited nervously in the reception of the hotel where the three were staying.

"Sir, we wondered where you'd gone," Blake said as Old Thomas returned from Babylon's Gates.

He looked at the pair of concerned faces before him and felt a rush of sympathy for them. He hadn't know where he was going himself and wasn't too sure what had happened. Then Jennings sniffed, rubbing his nose along his sleeve.

"Stop that at once, boy. It is of no concern to you where I have been. Go and ask the Station Master to alert me as soon as a Stranger named Justice enters the town. Blake, go and see Mr. Holland the funeral director and ask him to arrange a meeting between myself and the Priest concerning the Sermoner at this morning's funeral. We shall be staying a few extra days."

"But sir –"

"But me no buts, Jennings. Do as I say, do it now and do it well."

The two assistants hurried off on their errands, leaving Old Thomas standing alone in the centre of the hotel's reception. He looked around himself for a moment, then walked into the bar attached to the reception hall. Sitting on one of the high stools beside the bar, he waved the barman over.

"Yes sir?"

Old Thomas the undertaker sighed. For a full minute he debated with himself, then ordered a whisky. He wondered whether the decision to tell Jimmy Hayfield, Justice, of Hook's message or not would be as easy.

I, OF THE BEHOLDER

I

They came from one direction, heading slowly in another, a train of horses, wagons and people that made up one of the many tribes of Walkers who called the vast Sadducee Plains their homes. They talked no more than they had to, all their concentration fixed upon safely making the journey from where they were to where they would be. Each of them remained wary of the many dangers the quiet Plains could hold even for those who had lived among them for the entirety of their lives.

As dusk drew on, they selected a camp site in which to spend the night and, with the practiced ease of professionals, within half an hour the entire train was encamped. Horses had been fed, watered and stabled, meals had been eaten, children and old folk had been put to bed. Camp fires became meeting places for friends and relatives to put aside the cares of the Walk and to talk aimlessly, swap stories and jokes, relax before the morning and the inevitable continuation of the trail.

The Walkers had no one leader, rather a collection of men and women who excelled in their chosen fields and who were accorded respect from those others who would learn from them. On some nights, many of them would collect in an informal council around one fire and talk of the Walkers and the Walk, comparing ideas and concerns that they may have. This evening, however, there was no such council, allowing the Walker Broken Horse, whom others sometimes called Father of the Plains, to join the fireside of his daughter One Feather and the Stranger who had Walked with the tribe for almost two years.

"Father, sit with us and take water." His daughter held out a bowl of water as Broken Horse sat beside her, which he took and drank from.

"Thank you daughter, I have taken water." He passed it back and they nodded and smiled to each other, the traditional greeting over. Broken Horse looked over at the Stranger who sat cross legged opposite him, his black, wide brimmed hat pushed back on his head, his long dark overcoat collected beneath him to serve as a cushion, his pistol laid beside him in its holster, a straight hanging from his lips, the end charred but unlit, his eyes staring off into nowhere. Eventually he noticed Broken Horse and One Feather staring at him and smiled, straightening himself up.

"Sorry, I was miles away."

"Indeed you were, Slake. Anywhere special?"

The Stranger shrugged. "No, not really. Just letting my mind wander."

"Our people say that if you let your mind wander long enough, someone else's mind will find your body empty and take it."

"From what I've learned, Horse, your people seem to have sort some sort of saying for just about everything." He fished in his waistcoat pocket for matches to relight his straight. "I wouldn't be surprised," he said smiling at the old man, "if you had some sort of homily about lighting up."

Broken Horse and his daughter laughed gently.

"No, Slake, I do not," he raised a finger and said, "But give me until morning and I'm sure I could find one."

"I bet you could," Slake said, cupping his hands around the end of his straight as he lit it. Pale blue smoke rose into the clear night sky, momentarily obscuring the stars and moons as he looked at them, before it was taken by the wind and pulled apart. He looked back at Broken Horse. "Have you met the new Stranger yet?"

"But of course. I am one of the Respected. I met him the second day after he joined us."

"What do you make of him?" Slake asked, dragging on his smoke.

Broken Horse sighed. "Well, I do not think he will bring us as much luck as yourself, but at least there is no bad will in his heart."

"What is his name, Father?" One Feather asked, picking at a bowl of dried fruit near the fire.

"He has taken the name of Crank," he said with a smile. Looking over at Slake he continued, "Perhaps not the best name I have heard a Stranger give himself, but as we say, each takes his own course."

"I don't suppose you'll be surprised if I tell you I'm thinking of leaving?" Slake asked.

"No, it would not surprise me. We will be sad to see you leave. You have brought us much good fortune in the time you have been with us. But as I have said, each takes his own course. When would you leave?"

"Well, we're almost at the Western edge of the Plains now. The Mainland Kingdoms are over to the South and West, so I guess I'll head off there tomorrow. Shouldn't take me long to clear the Plains, maybe another day or so."

Broken Horse nodded his head. "It was kind of you to wait until another Stranger joined us. I know you have been wanting to leave for several weeks now."

"Least I could do, Horse. I know how you people like to have at least one Stranger travelling with you. Now you've got this Crank guy," the three smiled at each other. "Well, I reckon it's time for me to move on."

Broken Horse lifted the bowl of dried fruit and handed it across to Slake.

"We will be sad to see you leave, Slake. Eat of our fruit freely, know that you are always welcome among our tribe and may your Judas Christ go with you."

"First two I'll take gladly, Horse. Last one you can keep if it's all the same to you."

The old man replaced the bowl of fruit after Slake had taken his fill and looked down at it, his fingers idly stirring the pieces of Soo's apple, blue beans and pale berries around the wooden container. Eventually, he looked back at Slake.

"You have never appeared to be concerned with the Strangers' god, Slake. Why is that?"

He shrugged, staring at the fire first, then at Broken Horse.

"I can't find it in my heart to believe in Christ, Horse. All the Judan Preachers say you have to have faith in Christ, to believe that he was hanged from that elder tree for you, but I can't do it."

"There are more gods than Judas, Slake. In the Blue States to the South, worship of the Lady of The Hills is more common than that of your Christ. Throughout the Mainland Kingdoms and even far to the North, beyond the realm of the Clansmen, the Cuckoo God is worshipped. To the West, the Funeral Wastes are laden with the spawn and followers of R'lyeh. It is said for every point on the compass there is a God."

Slake flicked ash from his straight into the fire, staring into the glowing embers, then looked up at Broken Horse.

"You'll have to excuse my scepticism, Horse. I find it hard enough to believe in the accepted god of Strangers, let alone any others."

"If you find that difficult to believe, how will you cope with the thought that there are more Strangers than Judas that have become gods?" The Stranger raised an eyebrow at the old man. "Do not look at me that way," Broken Horse said in mock anger. "I would not lie to you. As I have said, more than one Stranger, like Judas Christ, has taken on the role of god and begat their own religion. Others have elected to stay here upon the Land to live on as Strangers."

"Gods living as Strangers?" Slake said with a shake of his head.

"Your doubt is commendable, Slake, but I have been witness to such things. You have to be willing to listen to things beyond your scepticism."

Slake looked across at One Feather who had been listening silently to their conversation. "Is there any chance of a drink, Feather? Something tells me this might be a long night."

She smiled at him, stood and went to her tent, returning a few minutes later with a flagon of water and three earthenware mugs. Sitting down next to Slake, she poured them each a drink, handing one to her father and one to Slake.

"Okay, Horse," Slake said, "I'm listening."

II

There are dark corners in this Land. We Walkers have known many different countries and many different peoples: the wild Clansmen of the cold Northern reaches where guns and pistols are unknown and where they use swords to settle their disputes; the people of the Southern countries whose culture is completely alien to ours, relying as they do upon mechanical wonders that defy description. The Mainlands are where we have chosen to roam, settling, if one may call it that, along the vast tracts of the Sadducee Plains. To the East lie the Frontier towns where the cult or religion of Judas Christ has taken root as nowhere else. To the West lay the Mainland Kingdoms and beyond them the vastness of the Funeral Wastes. We have attempted to find some sort of mid–ground, a form of neutral territory that we may call our own, as far as any creature may lay claim to the Land. Many people would believe that we have seen the light of the sun shine upon all there is to see in this Land of ours. And yet, there are dark corners.

One such place lays to the East of the Frontiers, bordering the range of hills and mountains that form the natural barrier to the

Land which lays beyond. There is a town there, perhaps the earliest town that the Natives built as they travelled West from over the mountains. The inhabitants called it Saramago, but it was also known as Far Reach. Few Natives travel there, now, and it has been many a year since a tribe of Walkers have ventured that far East.

There was once a great deal of trade between the Walkers and the Natives of Saramago – we would bring them news and goods from the Mainland Kingdoms and the Frontiers and in return they would furnish us with minerals and animal hides that we could trade with the Natives further West. Though the earliest Judan settlers had built the town, the religion had faltered; the true believers had continued West, bearing their tales of the Lost Stranger. They took with them other things, too. They claimed to own the One True Noose that had been placed around the neck of Christ and which could cure the sick and infirm. They also claimed to have the Sword of Fate which had been used to pierce Christ's side as he hung from the tree. This sword, they said, could kill a god, stained as it was with the blood of a divine being.

As time went by, however, the people of Saramago came to think of those tales as we do – as being just tales, nothing more. They were not simple folk, and as such they felt no need for faith in a person they knew only through stories. They worshipped no gods of their own, though they thanked the Seasons for the full harvest and the good growing, and to whom they submitted for the drought and snow. They had no need for gods until the coming of the Stranger named Fugue.

In my sixth year, our tribe camped in Saramago for two Seasons, and in that time came a lone man, a Stranger from across the mountains. No one, to the knowledge of the Natives of Saramago, had emerged from the Eastern side of the mountains since the first settlers some seventeen hundred years before. The Land beyond was unknown to them and, as far as I know, to any other, and yet the Stranger named Fugue walked down from the summits and into the town. There is no Station for Strangers in that town as there is in others, and the Natives had no idea of how to deal with his appearance. It seemed only logical for them to ask us to take the Stranger into our tribe, which we did, offering to him the same hospitality that we gave to the Stranger who was travelling with us at that time. With the wonder that is hindsight, it is easy to wish we had not.

Such was the confusion caused by the arrival of the Stranger from the Eastern side of the mountains that a Council of Respecteds was called. My grandfather sat upon that Council in the highest esteem, as he had done for many years before and did for many after. The Eldermen, Native leaders of the town of Saramago, sat with the Respecteds on that Council, the first time that such an event had happened, and the Stranger known as Fugue was called to meet them in the great tent that was erected only when the Council was called. Many of the Walkers and Natives of Saramago huddled and jostled for space to watch the proceedings.

After keeping the Council waiting for almost half an hour, the Stranger named Fugue entered the tent and stood before the gathered people.

"What is it that you would have of me?" he asked in a proud voice.

"We would know where it is you come from and what your intentions towards our peoples are," the Council responded.

"Why should I answer these questions?" Fugue replied. "Can you not accept that I am a mere traveller heading from one place to another? Who calls you Walkers into account when you happen to meet a town?"

The Council, unused to being questioned, paused.

"No—one since the earliest times has descended from the mountains," one of the Eldermen said. "We are curious and wish to know where it is you come from."

"I shall tell you from whence I came," Fugue stated, turning around to face the Walkers and Natives that had gathered in the tent. "I am sent down as Herald to the Man in the Silver Mountain, he who is the Nexus and Focal Point, he who is both Eye and Beholder, King and Fool. I am both Herald and Servant of the Celestial Jester who is known beyond the mountains as both Beginning and Ending, One Point and All Points, Loci and Locus. It is he that has sent me down into this Land of yours to bring to you his Message."

"What is this message?" the Council of Respecteds asked.

"The Message that he is the Way," Fugue said, speaking all the while to the crowd.

"The way to what?" someone shouted. Fugue turned his gaze to the caller.

"The Way to everlasting salvation. It is only through Loci that you may continue through this sordid pit that is your lives. Embrace him, allow him free entrance to your homes and he will visit you, bringing freedom from the iniquities of your pathetic existence. He will lift you to a higher plane, allowing you to climb the mountain that is his home to enter into his presence and be rewarded for your servitude to him. Not in some vague, otherworldly state as other gods have offered, but while you live, in the here and now as he is the Here and Now, the Once and Forever god who will play as you do, who will punish as you do. Do not wait till death for salvation, for Loci offers it now! He cares not for any other gods you may have. He has fought Great R'lyeh and won! The Cuckoo God will not face him! Judas Christ has paid him homage! He asks not for your repentance, merely your allegiance! He does not want to take your souls as empty vessels, he would rather you offer them while they still reside in your bodies! Pledge your troth unto he who is both Master and Servant and you shall be gifted not only after your death, but while you yet live!"

Such was the fervour of Fugue's call that many in the crowd cheered at the close of his speech. The Council of Respecteds began to ask him more of this Celestial Jester, this Loci, but he ignored them, instead appealing to the baser levels of the crowd.

He offered them riches both spiritual and physical in the realm of Loci if they would but follow him in his imminent return to the mountain kingdom of his Lord.

The people of Saramago were poor folk for all their intelligence. Had they been fools perhaps they would have taken more persuading. It is easier to fool a man who feels himself intelligent, than it is to fool a feeble minded man who is ingrained in his ways and less susceptible to change. The promise of riches both monetary and religious set their minds alight as nothing else had done. The tales of the Judan god, stern and demanding in his ways, had long since lost their appeal and no other god had managed to win them over. This one man's talk of a god who would accept anyone who would join him, regardless of station or piety, appealed to the laziness of their souls. Why should they toil and strive to be good and kind in the hope of being rewarded after they died, when apparent salvation was before them in the shape of Fugue, Herald of Loci?

And yet, they were not all swayed. A woman named Ruth, who was one of the Eldermen, raised her voice against Fugue.

"And where is your proof, Stranger?" she cried. We Walkers were dismayed to hear that after only one speech, some of her own townsfolk jeered her, siding already with this Herald. "Show us something of your god's powers that we may judge with an open mind whether we should accept him or you into our homes."

"You wish proof woman?" Fugue said, still not turning round to face the Council or the Eldermen. "What would you have me do? Turn your neighbours into toads?" The crowd before him laughed, somewhat nervously, at his apparent joke. "You, woman!" he cried suddenly, pointing into the crowd. The people jostled each other until a clear space had formed around the twisted, shrunken form of a woman who appeared old before her time and leaned heavily on a stick. "Come here, be the test that this town needs."

The woman looked around herself nervously, but her gaze

would not be met by any of her townsfolk around her. Haltingly, she limped towards Fugue who now had the attention of everyone in the tent.

"Come here, crone," he said. She stood before him, trembling with fear, mute with excitement, as he put his hand on her forehead and looked up to the roof of the tent and the sky beyond.

"Locus! Loci! Give your humble servant the strength to remove the affliction from this woman's body, the unholy ailment that makes me gag with its stench!" He gave a great cry, his back contorting, his body writhing in all manner of forms until he wrenched his hand away from the woman's head and staggered back, cradling his arm as if it had been burned.

The woman stood, unchanged, unmoving.

"It would seem your god has decided not to answer your call," Ruth said smugly. Fugue turned to look at her for the first time and, from where I sat, I saw him give her such a look as gave me nightmares for weeks. His eyes danced and sparkled, his red tongue lolled from his mouth longer than any normal man's should, his teeth shone and appeared sharp and pointed as if they'd been filed. He pointed back to the woman, grinning at Ruth, as if she had just provided the prompt he needed.

The woman screamed as her back straightened suddenly, her arms flying out at right angles to her body, the walking stick shooting through the air to land amongst the crowd, her whole form raised up on her toes for a full minute till she collapsed to her knees. Someone from the crowd called out her name, "Mary! Mary!" and made as if to run to her, but stopped when the woman retched violently, holding her stomach as the contents of her innards vomited themselves upon the floor.

And what contents they were. Vile, black forms, glistening with juices from the woman's body, rolled about on the floor, their slim tentacles and misshapen limbs slapping wetly, attempting to gain purchase. Staring, vacuous eyes swam in sockets that would collapse around them and appear elsewhere, and wailing, open mouths poured out the inhuman sounds of their agony as they were aborted, forcibly birthed from their host. The crowd screamed as one, yet remained standing, held there, watching the spectacle of these creatures that had just emerged from a woman most of them knew, and who lay slumped to one side, a thin trickle of blood running from her mouth and a small pool of urine beneath her legs.

Fugue stepped forward and grabbed the things in his hands. No—one was certain how many of the things there were as they constantly moved and crawled over and into each other, but he picked them up and held them in his clenched fists.

"Here is the proof of Loci who is Locus!" he cried, waving the still crying things to the crowd. "Here is the power of my god to work miracles!" he cried, allowing all to see. "Here is the strength of my god!" And with that, he crushed the black creatures in his hands, and still to this day I sometimes hear the sick, wet sound as their bodies burst open in his grasp.

The crowd were hushed, the expression on their faces a mixture of disgust and awe as they watched the fetid remains pour from between Fugue's fingers. He wiped the sickly flesh from his hands then walked over to the woman Mary and knelt beside her still form.

"Come, woman. Your affliction has been removed by the power of the Man in the Silver Mountain. Stand. Walk. Live." He stood up and moved away from her as she raised her head, coughing the last of the bile and blood from her mouth. Pushing up with her hands, she sat back on her legs, looking around for her stick.

"Come, woman," Fugue repeated. "Come. Walk."

She stared at him for a moment, her gaze seeming to see nothing except the Stranger, and then, to the gasped amazement of the crowd, the woman rose, unsteady at first, then with growing certainty, until she stood unaided for the first time in years. Fugue turned and spoke to the Council of Respecteds and the Eldermen as one for the first time.

"Here is the proof you asked for," he said indicating Mary. "My god, who would be yours if you desire, has granted your boon. Having demonstrated his power, I will now leave you and retire to my tent, allowing you to discuss whatever it is you feel you have to." He smiled then, a wicked, mocking smile and bowed low before them, turned, and walked from the Council.

As we Walkers watched, the Natives of Saramago hovered uneasily, unsure of what to do, until Mary followed her healer down the aisle and into the sunshine. At first, only a few went after her, but, as with a dam that breaks, once there is a trickle, the flood will soon follow and so it was with the townspeople. More and more filed out of the tent, taking with them some of us Walkers, until only the main body of Walkers and the Council remained.

There was little said following Fugue's departure. The Council of Respecteds decided, in the characteristic manner of we Walkers, that until Fugue performed a violent act against one of our own, we would continue to harbour him in his tent. The Eldermen of Saramago worried and doubted him, disliking the immediate power he had assumed over most of the Natives through his rhetoric, and they urged us to remove him from our company.

It was my grandfather who insisted that Fugue had done nothing wrong. Indeed, he argued, he had only done good by curing the woman Mary of her disease. Admittedly, the people of Saramago appeared to be fascinated by him, but that was only to be expected – he was a Stranger, a healer and magician and he claimed to be the herald of some god in the mountains. Soon, my grandfather reasoned, the people would become tired of him and only a very few, if any at all, would join him in his return to his god Locus who was also called Loci and a lot of other names.

The Eldermen were appeased by my grandfather's talk, listening to him with the blind respect they gave to the man who was the closest thing to an overall leader of our tribe. Only Ruth dissented, she who had demanded proof from Fugue. She claimed that the fascination that Fugue held over the townsfolk was not mere curiosity, but a glamour, a spell placed upon them by this Stranger from East of the Mountains. In those times, when I was a child, sorcery was far easier to find and believe in than in these chill days, and Strangers were more often seen to perform wizardry than shoot somebody. My grandfather, however, despite his own belief in sorcery, disagreed with Ruth, saying that over the next day or two, the people of Saramago would become bored with Fugue as he ceased to be anything unusual and became just another Stranger with a little magic and a new god.

Swayed by his argument, the other Council members and the Eldermen ignored Ruth's still adamant claims of sorcery and retired to their respective homes. And I, the small child of six that had witnessed all this from the shadowy corners? I went home also, albeit not with any great enthusiasm, for the sights of the day still danced and slithered wetly behind my eyes in the theatre of my mind. As I walked towards my family's tent, I passed nearby to the tent of Fugue and saw him standing outside talking with a man who stood six feet tall and was made even taller by the strange three pointed hat he wore. Two points went out from the sides of his head while the last reached up from the top, each of them curved at the ends and capped with small bells. Both the hat and his clothes − a simple jacket and breeches − were made of mismatched patches of green and red cloth; they were not ordered enough to be called alternating, but looked instead as if they had been simply thrown together. I made no noise, standing quite still in order to catch their conversation with the hungry, curious ear of a six year old, but as I listened, the tall man turned and stared at me.

"Go to your family's tent, Rainbow Beard's Son," he said with a smile. I was not to become Broken Horse until my thirteenth birthday. "My business is not with you this day," he said and threw his head back and laughed which made the bells that hung at the points of his hat ring and jingle, a sane and musical accompaniment to the insanity that seemed to be at the soul of his laughter.

Needless to say, I ran as fast as my small legs could carry me.

63

After three days had passed, the townsfolk had still not become bored with Fugue or his message. Instead, if it were possible, it seemed that even more had become interested and camped daily outside his tent, entering in ones or twos to be told various secret things that they would not reveal to anyone. Ruth again tried to convince the other Eldermen and Respecteds that they should remove him before too much damage was done, but once again, my grandfather had the final word. He conceded that the people had not yet lost interest, and that it appeared more were being enticed by the Stranger's talk. But, he insisted, this state of affairs could not last. The people of Saramago were intelligent people and, sooner or later, they would come to realise the error of their ways and return to the day to day life that they should be leading.

Again, with the wisdom that is hindsight, I can look back clearly and see that my grandfather, in his old age, had become used to being regarded as the leader of the Walkers and disliked having his decrees questioned. I doubt that he would have admitted it had anyone been bold enough to tell him, however. Pride is a strange thing. I believe my grandfather wished to be obeyed, to keep the waters of life still and to live out his last days in peace and quiet, to keep everything going as if nothing new was happening, hence his reticence to evict Fugue.

The next day, four days after he had appeared from the mountains, Fugue returned from whence he came. This would have pleased Ruth and the other Eldermen had the Stranger not elected to take over three quarters of the townsfolk with him.

As the sun rose from behind the mountains, a vast trail of people emerged from the houses of Saramago, and a few from the tents of our tribe. At their head was the Stranger Fugue and the woman whom he had cured, Mary. With backpacks stuffed full of food and possessions, the train began to move, heading towards the mountains. Children, both those of the townsfolk who were making the trek and those of the Walkers who saw the whole thing as a game, followed them, running in and out of the line of people. So it was that I was near the head of the column when they were greeted by Ruth.

"What are you doing with these people?" she asked Fugue.

"Taking them to meet their new god," the Stranger replied simply and quietly, all the fervour of his speech in the Council tent gone.

"You cannot. The town will die without them."

"But they will live without the town," Fugue countered. "And how could you stop us? We leave of our own free will, to go where we will."

Ruth stared past Fugue at the men and women who had been her friends and neighbours and who stared back at her with angry faces. She was in their way, impeding their march to enlightenment. She hung her head, knowing that nothing she said would make any difference to them now. Fugue grinned at her as he had in the tent, his eyes all aglow and his teeth, suddenly seeming large and hungry, gleaming in the early morning light. As Ruth stepped to one side, defeated, Fugue and his party started forward.

I and some of the other children watched them go, gradually getting smaller as they neared the foothills of the mountains until we could hardly see them. Most of the other children drifted back into the empty town or to the Walkers' tents, but I sat across the road from where Ruth still stood. When I could no longer see the group of converts, I turned to look at the lone woman, the only one who, for some reason of her own, had defied Fugue as much as she could. I did not know, at the time, why she had done so. As my grandfather had said, Fugue had done nothing wrong, and the people that had followed him had done so of their own choice, for all Ruth's talk of glamour and sorcery. Why had she disliked him so? Had I been older, I may have attempted, at least, to find out. As it was, my answers appeared behind her dressed in the same outfit of mismatched green and red cloth as before, a three pointed hat on his head, bells at the end of each point.

The jester emerged from the shadows and walked over to Ruth who turned and looked at him with no real surprise.

"What will you do with them?" she asked.

"Ah, my dear, sweet Judith. Ever the innocent, eh?" His arm went around her shoulder and, not unkindly, pulled her close and hugged her. "You know that I will not answer that, yet each time you ask it."

"And each time you never answer."

He sighed and melodramatically placed the back of his free hand against his forehead. In it he held a short stick at the top of which was a stuffed miniature version of his own head and hat, complete with bells.

"Oh Judith," he cried forlornly, "would you take all my secrets from me even as you have taken my heart?" He fell gracefully and slowly to the floor and lay, both hands over his chest. "My heart is yours, Judith, you know that, yet my secrets are mine own, my burden."

"Get up," she said, still staring in the direction that Fugue and the townsfolk had taken. With a laugh, the jester flipped himself up on to his feet and capered around her. "Stop it," she snapped. He stood in front of her, his head low in a mockery of repentance. "Why do you do this?"

"You know the answer to that only too well, my love, my sweet, my darling darkling. The answer is obvious if only you would pluck out your eyes and look with your heart. Fugue is my Herald at this time. Every time this story is told, more people will hear of him, the mysterious magical Herald who can cure the sick. And as more hear of him, more will hear of the mystical maniacal Fool whom he serves, he who is known as Loci and Locus, One Place and All Places. Every soul that comes to me is one less for the Lady of The Hills, the Cuckoo God, the Christ, R'lyeh, the Land Lord, the Nameless One or any of the others. In this way will the path be laid for my arrival. Each telling of this tale is another stone on the path that leads from my door

66

ever onward into the realms of all men, Native, Walker, Stranger, Clansman and more. That is why I do this, and that is why I make you do this."

Ruth stared up at him, somehow managing to look deep into the glowing pits that were his eyes.

"You truly are a fool," she said.

He screamed his laughter, hopping from foot to foot and holding his sides. "Yes, my love, my Judith, indeed I am, for only a fool would continue to love when there is none returned, and all the gods of all the Land know that I love you.

"But enough, we must away. I must spirit you into another town to fence against my Herald, whomever it be, when he next appears, and I must fly to my new found converts who even now approach my abode. So my sweetest, dearest thing," he bent and kissed her hand. "I bid you a fond farewell, a good journey, a new identity and a complete loss of memory until we meet again."

And with that, she vanished. No grand spells, no theatrics, she merely vanished. I sat in the shade of the porch from which I had witnessed all this, my eyes wide and in danger of falling out. My condition was not helped when the jester turned to me and smiled the same glowing smile Fugue had used against Ruth who the jester had called Judith.

"You truly are a persistent boy, Rainbow Beard's Son, but as I said, my business is not with you this day. Go, remember what you have seen and heard and tell it to those who will listen. One day I will see you again."

He bowed to me, turned towards the mountains, bent his knees and jumped, vanishing into the air accompanied by a clap of what sounded like thunder. I sat for perhaps five minutes, disbelieving my own eyes, then stood and walked into the street, over to where they had stood. The ground was covered in the footprints of Fugue's followers, but the jester's last prints were clear enough. His large, pointed boots had left two deep, clear impressions where he had jumped from. I looked up into the sky, but saw nothing except a few clouds.

III

"**W**hat happened then?" Slake asked. Broken Horse turned his gaze away from the fire and looked sadly at the Stranger.

"That is always the question at the end of an unsatisfactory tale, my friend. What happened then was, quite simply, that I ran to join the rest of the Walkers and tell them what I had seen and heard, but everyone seemed too busy to listen. I wandered among our tents for the four more days that we stayed in Saramago, wondering about Fugue and the Jester and Ruth whom he had called Judith. Then, when we moved onwards, the whole incident seemed less important, and I put it aside. It was almost five years before I told someone the story."

"Who was he, father? The Jester, I mean?" One Feather asked.

"I do not know, my child. We Walkers have long believed that the easiest way to tell the difference between a liar and a truthsayer is that the liar always has the answers at the end of his story, while the truthsayer must be forced to shrug his shoulders and admit that he does not know."

"So you have no idea who this Loci guy was?" Slake asked him, lighting up another straight. He was surprised to feel his legs had gone numb from sitting in the same position for so long and winced as he stretched them.

"I have my ideas, but no proof. I believe he was what both Fugue and he claimed him to be: a god. I have met perhaps a dozen people who have heard the tale, or at least a similar version, with the same characters of the Herald – though he is not always called Fugue – Loci and a woman who defies them, but set in different places. I have heard it set in Trevenna, one of the towns near the Funeral Wastes, as well as in the great city of Rollright in the Southern Lands. I have also met four other people who have witnessed the events, in much the same way that I did."

"People who have met this Jester?" One Feather asked. "What did they say?"

Her father shrugged. "They had their own ideas, as do I; more than that I could not say because they did not," he looked at them both. "Listen to me, this is important: tales such as I have told cannot ever end satisfactorily. Only a fool would try to tie up the loose ends. I cannot say what fate befell those townspeople who followed Fugue, because I do not know. These tales are a reflection of life, they are the mirror of experience. One cannot go through life without encountering events that, to oneself at least, appear to have no meaning, no reason and the outcome of which one never learns. Such are these tales. It is a foolish man indeed who expects to learn all the secrets at the end of the tale. It cannot be done, except by the best of liars, and even then their secrets are lies."

Broken Horse hung his head and gazed at the fire.

"It is late. We should go to our beds," he stood slowly, with his daughter's help. "I will see you before you leave, Slake," he said to the Stranger, nodded a goodnight to him and headed for his tent.

"I suppose he's right," Slake said, throwing the remains of his straight into the fire. "No—one ever finds out what really happens in the end."

"I think we all know what happens in the end," One Feather said. "Come," she said, holding out her hand. "Let's go to bed."

IV

Two days later, Slake stood facing West in the scrub land that marked the end of the Sadducee Plains, and the beginning of the Mainland Kingdoms. Off to the South the rolling green continued unhindered for miles, until it joined the horizon, which was smudged by the dark growth of trees that, unless he was mistaken, marked the beginning of the great Penny's Forest. Far to the South West could be seen the outlying farms and hamlets that formed the suburbs of the city of Oxenford. He had been thinking of making for the city over the past day or so, since he had left Broken Horse, One Feather and the Walkers. The Sheriff there was a good man who was inclined to get on with Strangers, but for some reason Slake found his gaze wandering Westward. If memory served him right, there was an old friend out that way and, after spending the last couple of years with the Walkers, he found he wasn't quite ready for his own company just yet.

As his dusty boots started down the last dune, kicking sand ahead of him over the dark, stunted grass that fought against the drier land, he wondered about Broken Horse's story of Strangers becoming gods. He wondered what would happen in the end.

THE CALM BEFORE

"That'll be the kid now," Exit said pushing his chair back and standing up. Taking one of the lanterns that hung around the room, he headed out on to the porch, holding the light high to illuminate as much ground as possible. In the glow of the oil lamp the small yard appeared sickly and sterile, the hard–packed dirt hostile and unwelcome. At the edge of the yard stood a wooden picket fence and a little further beyond lay the stable.

The horse that Exit had heard trotted up to the stable and stopped, the rider dismounting immediately. He raised his hand to Exit to show that he had seen him, then took his horse into the stable to tend to her. Exit waited on the porch for the few minutes that it took for the rider to stable his horse, then the older man watched as he walked to the house, pulling his leather gloves off, his back pack slung over one shoulder.

"Whose are the other horses?" the young rider asked as he stepped up on to the porch.

"Friends of mine, a couple of Strangers I taught some years ago. Names are Slake and Dale."

The young rider swung his back pack off and held it by the straps, frowning at Exit. "Slake you say?"

"Ahuh. Come in and meet them. Did you get everything I asked you to?" Exit asked, indicating the pack.

"Yeah," the pair walked into the house, the rider turning right to enter the kitchen and drop the pack on to the work top before joining his teacher in the main room where he sat at the table with two Strangers.

"Slake, Dale," Exit said as he entered. "Like you both to meet my latest prodigy, name of Justice."

"Howdy," Dale said, raising his hand by way of greeting.

"Howdy Stranger," Slake said, holding out his hand. Justice stared at him for a moment, the atmosphere beginning to feel uncomfortable as the time stretched, Exit looking at Justice with a frown, until the young Stranger finally reached out and grasped Slake's forearm.

"I've just been telling them what a fine shooter you're turning out to be," Exit said, smiling with a quiet pride in his latest student's abilities. A Stranger like the others, he had taken it upon himself in his later years to teach those who would learn how to use the myriad types of pistols to be found in the Mainland Kingdoms, in the hands of Strangers and Natives, both good and bad.

Before he sat down, Justice took a glass from the cupboard behind him and placed it on the table in front of him. Sitting opposite Slake, he reached forward and took the opened bottle of whisky that stood beside the lantern and poured himself a drink.

"Do I know you from somewhere, Justice?" Slake asked. The neck of the bottle clattered against the glass as Justice spilt whisky and looked up at the Stranger across the table. Raising the glass to his lips he swallowed the entire contents in one go and slammed it back down on the table.

"I'd say that's a yes, mate," Dale said. Justice stared at Slake.

"Yes, you know me," he said quietly. "It's partly your fault that I'm here."

"Sorry?" Slake asked.

"What are you talking about, kid?" Exit said quietly, placing a hand on Justice's arm.

"Remember Kingston, Slake? Remember your friend Hook?"

"Looks like your past is catching up with you, Slake," Dale said with a grin.

"I remember Kingston, kid. What about it?"

"You remember some young kid telling you to get out when you refused to deal with Hook?" Slake looked closely at Justice, mentally comparing this Stranger's sun–tanned and wind blown face to the vague memory of years gone by, trying to ignore Justice's longer hair, feathered braid and dark stubble.

"Sweet Judas, it's you isn't it?"

"Yeah, it's me," Justice said, standing rapidly, his pistol already in his hand and levelling at Slake's head when Dale grabbed his gun hand and pushed him back against the wall, his own pistol tucked under the young Stranger's chin.

"What the Hell is going on here, kid?" Exit asked.

"That son of a bitch is the reason I became a Stranger," he said looking over at Slake, ignoring Dale. "That bastard wouldn't help us in Kingston so I had to stand up to Hook and he turned me into a Stranger."

"You got a messed up way of telling a story, kid," Dale said. "Now, do you feel like dropping the gun, sitting down and telling us what the Hell this is all about?"

Justice closed his eyes briefly and sighed, all the fight having left him, and let his pistol fall to the floor. Very carefully, Dale stepped back and allowed Justice to pass him and sit back at the table, reaching again for the bottle of whisky. Over his head, Exit and Dale swapped concerned looks, then went back to their seats.

"Tell me what happened, kid," Slake said gently. Justice raised his head to look across the table at Slake and grinned ruefully.

"What happened? That bastard Hook destroyed my life. Up until he came to town, I was a Native. My name was Jimmy Hayfield and I lived in a small Frontier town called Kingston. We had a few Strangers wander through there from time to time, one of which was dear old Slake here," Justice lifted his glass to the Stranger in an ironic salute. "Not long after he'd turned up this one Season, another Stranger, name of Hook, came into

73

town and started tearing the place up. After a while me and some of the other townsfolk got together and confronted Slake, wanting him to help us get rid of Hook. You remember what you said, Slake?"

"Can't say as I do, kid."

Justice poured himself another whisky. "I asked when you Strangers were going to start giving instead of taking, and you asked back 'When are you Natives going to stop depending on Strangers to do your dirty work?'" He paused for a few minutes, staring deep into his glass, as if reliving the moment. "You left soon after that, after I'd stupidly said that I'd deal with Hook. All I wanted was to get that lunatic out of my town. As things turned out, I've ended up on some dumb, stupid quest to find him."

"Just find him, kid?" Exit asked. "Or kill him."

"I have to find him at least, so I can find my parents."

Dale leaned forward. "Your parents? Now what are you talking about, kid?"

"The whole reason I became a Stranger, the whole purpose of this stupid quest is to find them. Find my parents," Justice looked at the quizzical faces around the table and sighed. "Hook and I fought. He beat me up and Judas knows what would have happened if some of the townsfolk hadn't helped. I owe those people my life and I can't even remember most of their names.

"Anyway, it seemed like the whole town ended up in the street outside the bar and I told Hook to get out of Kingston. The son of a bitch laughed at me, blood running down his face from where I'd broken his nose. He did something then, I don't know what, but the next thing I knew there was a circle of fire rising up to about ten feet or so, completely surrounding us, cutting the pair of us off from the others.

"'Sit down,' he said, all calm and collected and for some reason I felt compelled to do it, sitting down opposite him, the pair of us cross legged in this bloody great fire circle. He said 'You've no idea who your parents are, do you?' I didn't know how he knew but it was true. I'd been an orphan, brought up by people I thought were my parents until they told me the truth when I was fifteen. He drew a circle in the sand with his finger, then drew some symbols around it. 'Look,' he said and as I did, a picture formed in the circle between us. A man and a woman in their forties or fifties were working on a farm and I knew, just knew, they were my parents.

"'I know where they are, Jimmy. I know their names, their favourite colour, even what they had for supper last night.' Hook said. 'If you want to find them, you have to find me.' The next thing I knew, I was huddled in the street, my clothes and hair smouldering from the fire, and Hook had vanished."

Justice leaned back in his chair and rubbed wearily at his eyes. Dale and Exit looked at each other and then over at Slake who shrugged and poured himself a glass of whisky.

"Hook called you his friend at one point, Slake. Were you?"

"I don't know that we were ever friends, kid," he said. "The Hook that I knew was always a mean bastard, and from what you say it doesn't sound as if he's changed much either. We hung around together for a few Seasons at one point, but that was more because we were both headed to the same place. I always thought his magic was just illusions and lies; I doubt he told you the truth with that vision. It's more likely he told you what you wanted to hear. Are you still going to try to find him?"

"I have to," Justice said. "I have no choice."

Exit leaned forward, his arms crossed on the table. "Of course you do, kid. The people Hook showed you in that vision could have been anyone. Like Slake said, he could have been showing you just what you wanted to see," He glanced at Dale and Slake, knowing how weak his words sounded.

"It's too late," Justice said hanging his head. "I've come too far. For seven years now I've been a Stranger, walking from one place to another trying to find Hook. And now I know where he is," he paused and sipped at his whisky. "Back in a town called White Stone, before I came here to learn how to shoot, I saw somebody from Kingston, the undertaker. He had seen Hook a week or so before I got into town and Hook had left him with a message for me," Justice looked around at the other Strangers, smiling slightly. "He's tired of me chasing him. He wants this to end. The undertaker said he's running with the Ivory Gang in Anchorhead, up North. That's where I'll find him. That's where he's waiting for me."

"And what, you're going to chase up there after him?" Dale asked. "I don't know who the Hell is in this Ivory Gang, but if it's being run by that bitch with the army jacket it's not going to be easy, kid. And that's a bloody understatement."

"I've met Ivory. I know what she's like. That's the main reason I came here."

"You're not a real Stranger, kid," Exit said. "Slake, Dale and myself were never Natives as you were. You can change back."

"So where did you come from? What made you Strangers?" Justice asked. His teacher sat back in his chair, smiling over at Slake and Dale.

"It's . . . complicated, kid. But we have no families here, we were never Natives. You kill a Stranger, you don't have to worry about his brothers or sisters coming for you, because none of us have any. We're Strangers in the Land, and we have no choice in that, we don't get a chance to be different. You do. Give this thing up. Let the past go and start anew before it gets too late."

Slowly, as if the weight of the Land was balanced precariously upon his shoulders, Justice stood and retrieved his pistol from where it lay on the floor.

"It's already too late," he said, and left for his bed.

Exit stood on the porch the next morning waiting for Justice to lead his horse from the stable. As the young Stranger emerged with the grey mare in tow, Exit walked down the steps and across the yard to the fence.

"Where are the other horses?" Justice asked.

"Dale and Slake have moved on, heading South. Why don't

you follow them and give up this whole quest idea? Or stay here and finish up your training? There are still things I could teach you that would help against Hook."

Justice sighed. "Someone else once advised me to give up on the quest, an old woman I met who lived on the edge of Penny's Forest. I couldn't do it then, even though I'd only been searching for Hook for two years at that point. Now, five years after that? I don't think I have anything else to live for."

Exit shook his head then clapped his young protégé on the shoulder.

"If you must continue with this insanity then at least go with my blessing. I hope you settle this thing with your life intact, Justice. So long."

He watched Justice step back to his horse and mount easily. As he turned his horse around, he waved once to his teacher and rode off North heading for the town of Anchorhead, and Hook.

THE END, FOR NOW

Justice watched the hanging from the South gate of Anchorhead, a militia man holding the gate closed until it was over. Both of them looked down the street to the congregation outside the Station where a man sat on a horse, his hands tied behind his back, a noose around his neck, the rope stretching up to the makeshift gallows above him. On the raised porch of the Station, a short man with long, wild hair falling down his back, walked back and forth as he raved and shouted at the crowd, a copy of the Book in one hand.

"Did I not tell you these Strangers were heathens? Did I not spread the word amongst you, telling you never to talk to Strangers? Did I not warn against these practitioners of magic and witchery? And lo! Was I not proved right?" The Preacher pointed at the Stranger who sat on the horse. "You, so called Canyon, you are charged with bewitching the daughters of this town and leading them into licentiousness and harlotry! You have taken away that which Christ himself gave them, their pure innocent souls, and have thrown them unthinkingly into the pit! For that, Stranger, there can be only one punishment!"

The Preacher looked out at the crowd which shouted back as if on cue, "HANG HIM! HANG HIM!" The short man waited until the crowd had vented their anger, looking alternately between them and the Stranger who sat calmly on the horse.

When the cries for his death subsided, the Preacher continued.

"Canyon, Stranger of no abode, this town has sentenced you to death by hanging for the crimes of rape and sodomy and acts too vile to be named! Have you anything to say before you travel to the throne of Christ to be judged?"

The crowd fell silent, everyone eager to hear the Stranger's last pleadings for his life, to be witness to a heathen falling terrified before the righteous anger of their god. Instead, Canyon merely looked at the Preacher and said, "If there is a Hell other than this Land, sir, I dare say I shall see you there."

Denied of their pious joy, and having had their leader insulted, the crowd roared again for him to be hanged. The Preacher turned to his assistant who stood at the front of the horse, holding the reins. With a nod, the young man began pulling at the reins, walking the horse slowly forward. As the saddle slipped further from beneath Canyon, his legs clutched involuntarily at the flanks of the creature in an attempt to keep it beneath him for as long as possible until, with a final tug on the reins, the horse took a last step and Canyon swung free, his weight supported only by the rope around his neck. He kicked and struggled for a few minutes, his face darkening, his eyes bulging until, as his bladder opened, he gave a last gasp and hung still.

"Brethren," the Preacher said in a softer voice, no longer feeling the urge to shout. "Let our Lord Judas take the soul of this sinner into his bosom and there cleanse him and allow him eternal life after death. Amen."

With a murmured response, the crowd began to disperse, occasionally looking back over their shoulders at the dangling corpse as they went home or back to work or to the saloon, leaving the body of Canyon swinging gently in the breeze.

From the gate, Justice watched the Preacher's assistant walk off with the horse, presumably to the stables, while the short, long haired man of Christ went across the street and entered the Sheriff's office. The militia man looked up at Justice on his horse.

"You sure you want to come in here, Stranger? Folks ain't been too keen on your kind since the Reverend arrived."

"I'm looking for the Ivory Gang. They in town?"

The man tugged nervously at the yellow scarf that marked him as a member of Anchorhead's militia, the band of volunteers that manned the four gates, one at each point of the compass in the walls of the large town.

"Well, they passed through. Sheriff was mighty pleased they didn't stay more'n one night."

"Do you know where they went?"

"They left by the North gate is all I know. Only things up that way are the Maiden Hills and the Midnight Sea."

"Is there anything up there? A farm or hamlet? Somewhere they'd head for?"

The man scratched at his beard, grinning. "Oh sure, plenty of places. They could maybe camp up by the river, but the water there ain't too good. There's a couple of deserted farmsteads and an old Convent up there, too. There's an old port on the other side of the Hills, on the edge of the Sea that, far as I know, still takes folk North, out of the Mainland Kingdoms."

Justice looked down the street at the still swinging figure, the hanged man slowly becoming less defined as the shadows of early evening crept over the town.

"Open up." The militia man shrugged and unlocked the gate, opening it wide enough for Justice and his horse to ride through. "That the only Stranger's Station in town?" he asked pointing to the building where Canyon hung.

"Can't say I know of a town with more'n one. 'Cept maybe Jerusalem."

Nodding to him, Justice gently urged his horse down the street. As he rode through he noticed the few people on the streets watching him. They whispered to each other and pointed. They had hanged one Stranger only moments before, and now another had entered the town seemingly to take his place. Justice found himself wondering if this had been such a good idea after all. Lanterns were lit inside the

Station as he reined his horse in and looked at the lifeless body before him. The Stranger spun lazily in the dry wind, twisting and turning like a fly dangling from a spider's thread.

"We come out with a cord around us and go back in the same way."

Justice looked around at the speaker. Stood in the doorway of the Station, a jay hanging limply from his lips, was Dale, the Stranger Justice had met at Exit's farmstead.

"I thought you'd headed South?" Justice said, dismounting and tethering his horse to the rail.

"Maybe we should have. This town ain't exactly friendly to Strangers," he dragged on his jay, blowing blue smoke out as he looked at the hanged man before them. "Canyon would vouch for that if he could."

Justice stepped up on to the porch. "You said we. Is Slake with you as well?"

Dale raised an eyebrow at him. "If you're still determined to find this Hook fella and go up against his gang, well, Slake reckoned you could do with some help. Between you and me, I think he feels guilty for getting you into this."

"I don't need his guilt," Justice opened the door and walked inside, spurs jingling with each step. Dale took another couple of puffs at his jay, then pitched the stub into the street. As he stood watching the people watching him, the Preacher left the Sheriff's office and walked up the street to the hotel further along. His assistant ran out from the side of the Station, caught him up and talked frantically for a few seconds, pointing back at the building. The Preacher turned around and stared at Dale, who with a smile tipped his hat at him and laughed quietly as the Preacher stormed off, his lackey in tow.

Dale walked over to the corpse of the Stranger and carefully held it still.

"That Preacher's a bit of a bastard, ain't he fella?" he asked. "Yeah, I guess he is," he said in answer to himself. Turning, he opened the door and stepped inside.

"Thought you could do with some help," Slake said.

Justice stared at him, unsure whether to be angry or not. Instead, he turned to the clerk at the desk and pulled the register toward him. Taking the pen and ink offered him, he wrote the date, his name and the last town he had visited, then thrust it back.

"I don't know whether I want your help," he said. Slake shrugged and settled himself deeper into the comfortable chair he sat in.

"Well, the offer's there, kid."

"Are you really dumb enough to go up against this Hook fella if he's running with Ivory and her gang?" Dale asked as he stepped inside. Justice turned to him.

"My argument is with Hook. I don't want to deal with the others."

Dale turned to the clerk. "The Ivory Gang passed through here a while back, didn't they?"

"Sure did. Damn glad they only stayed one night an' all. Sons of bitches tore up –"

"How many were there?" Dale asked, interrupting him.

"Four all told. Meanest Strangers I've seen in –"

"What were there names?" The clerk hmmphed and flicked through the register.

"Ivory, Hook, Rune and Chain," he said sharply.

"You think those others are just going to let you have a go at their buddy and not get involved?" Dale asked Justice.

"The only one I've any business with is Hook."

Slake chuckled to himself. "The more I hear, the more I'm sure you need our help, kid. We both know Hook can be a bit wild, and I've heard this Rune ain't exactly the sort of guy who'll let you have a go at someone who's riding with him."

"And I know Ivory can be a real bitch, and Chain's just plain crazy," Dale said. "Met him near the Funeral Wastes once."

Justice looked at the pair of them. "Fine. You want to get involved in this, that's up to you. Either way, myself and Hook are going to sort this thing out once and for all." He turned to the clerk and asked for his room key and his horse to be stabled. "Right now, all I'm going to do is get some rest," he said and headed for the stairs.

"What he's going to do is get his head blown off," Dale said.

"So, where to, kid?" Slake asked Justice the next morning. They sat with Dale around a table drinking coffee, the only Strangers in the Station. Justice sighed.

"I spoke with one of the militia men last night as I came into town. Ivory and her gang left Anchorhead a few days back by the North gate. There's a bunch of hills beyond the town where they could be hiding out, then there's the Midnight Sea."

"Won't they have just sailed away?" Dale asked.

"No. Hook left a message for me telling me to come here, to Anchorhead, to sort things out. If he's hiding in the hills I'd rather get to him first than have him come here and catch us unawares."

"You've obviously been thinking about this, kid," Slake said. "What's our first move?"

Justice sighed and sipped at his coffee. "Pay a visit to the Sheriff. Find out if he knows of anywhere they could be hiding out. If he knows some places, we check them out. If he doesn't, we ride out into the hills and see what we can find ourselves."

"You know," Dale said leaning back in his chair. "The more I think about this, the crazier it seems. You and Slake both know this Hook guy, and you both agree he's a madman, and something of a wizard to boot. I've met Chain and the guy must have been dropped on his head at birth. Slake's said this Rune guy's also completely off his head, and I think we all know about Ivory, and she's running the bunch so she's got to be worse than the rest of them."

Justice grinned at Dale. "She is. I've met her." He stood,

putting his hat on. "I'm gonna head over to the Sheriff's place. You want to come along?"

"No, we'll stay here, kid. Let us know what you find out."

Justice nodded and left, stepping out into the early morning sun. Dale looked over at Slake.

"What the Hell are we getting ourselves into here? Me, you and some kid who's only just learned how to shoot a pistol properly going up against four crazy Strangers. Seems to me we're just a different kind of crazy."

"Maybe we are, my friend. But I kinda got the kid into this, so I'm gonna try and help him out. You don't have to come along."

Dale shook his head with a resigned smiled. "Hell, I ain't doing anything else right now. Suppose I'll hang around. Hopefully not like Canyon, though."

The Sheriff looked up as Justice entered his office, took his feet off the table and stood up.

"Howdy, Stranger," he said, straightening his hat and trying to hold his paunch in. Justice looked him up and down, managing to hide the contempt in his eyes. The man who stood before him had to be the oldest town Sheriff he had ever seen in all his years of travelling. Sixty if he was a day, overweight and unkempt, he was hardly a figure to instil either respect or fear.

"Sheriff," Justice said, tipping his hat. "I'm looking for the Ivory Gang. Heard they passed through here a while back."

"Sure, sure they did. None too sad to see 'em go either," the Sheriff indicated the seat near Justice and took his own behind the desk. Reaching down into an open drawer, he pulled out a bottle of cheap whisky and a couple of glasses. "Drink, Stranger?"

"Any idea where they went?" Justice asked, still standing. The Sheriff hesitated for a second, poured himself a shot of whisky then placed the bottle back in the drawer.

"I hope there ain't gonna be trouble, Stranger?" he asked carefully.

"I'm not looking for trouble. I'm looking for the Ivory Gang. The militia man on the South gate last night said they'd headed North into the hills. You know of anywhere they may have headed for?"

The Sheriff ran his hand across his stubble. "I wouldn't know for sure; we were just glad they passed through," he leaned forward, resting his elbows on the desk, his glass still in his hand. "We don't want any gun fighting in this town, Stranger. We keep ourselves to ourselves, see? Last thing us Natives want is a bunch of Strangers shooting the place up."

Justice smiled and looked down at the Sheriff.

"Unless I find out where they went, we may well end up fighting in this town. So if you can think of anywhere they might be hiding . . . ?"

The Sheriff finished his whisky. "About a couple of miles North into the Maiden Hills there's the old Convent of Saint Mary. It's been abandoned for the last ten or twelve years, give or take, since the Cynian–Aymian wars. Seems like the most likely place."

"Thank you Sheriff," Justice turned to go, then paused at the door. "One last thing; who's the Preacher in town?"

The Sheriff grinned. "That's the Reverend Ronald John Diver, come up North out of the Blue States. You don't want to mess with him, Stranger, less you want to end up swinging from a rope like that Canyon fella outside the Station."

"Reverend Diver, eh?" Justice said, smiling himself. "Well, well." He tipped his hat at the Sheriff again and headed back to the Station.

Staring out at the street from his hotel window, the Reverend saw Justice leave the Sheriff's office and cross into the Station opposite. Letting the curtain fall back across the window, he turned to his manservant who stood patiently next to the bed.

"It seems the Lord Judas calls us into his service once more, William. It would appear that the good Sheriff Tidyman has been consorting again with the Strangers housed in that infernal Station. My hat and coat if you would."

Opening a cupboard, William brought out the Reverend's long black coat and small brimmed hat, helping him put them on. As the Reverend left the room, William quickly grabbed his own coat and rushed after him. The other guests in the hotel watched the pair walk through the lobby, most of whom called out to him with adoration in their voices. There were only a few who barely managed to suppress smiles behind their hands and who considered the Reverend to be a pompous fool, far too full of himself to allow any room for Judas Christ.

The Reverend paid no attention to either group, but hurried through the hotel and out into the dusty street that was just coming to life with people going about their business. Men tended to horses in the stables, the postman delivered letters, the women of the town with their children now in the school building, walked along, collecting groceries and chatting with each other.

"I swear, William, that our curse is that of sociability. If we Natives did not feel the urge to congregate in such numbers, half our problems would be over instantly. Small villages are the answer. A strictly controlled birth rate. Keep the populace in control. Allow no religion other than that of Judas. When Christ said 'I am the Way', this was the way he referred to."

William walked behind the Reverend, trying to remember his words so that he could write them down as soon as they returned to their rooms at the hotel. Soon, his master would have a large enough collection of sermons and musings to publish another book.

"Morning Reverend," the Sheriff said from his doorway, standing up straight and taking off his hat as the Reverend climbed the steps up on to his porch.

"Sheriff Tidyman. May we talk inside?"

"Well, why don't we just talk out here, Reverend? Looks to be a lovely day. Best make the most of the good weather while we got it. Christ knows it's rare enough this early in the Season."

Tbnhe Reverend stood patiently before him until the Sheriff coughed and moved to one side, allowing the Preacher and his manservant to enter his office. Once they were all inside, the Sheriff sat in the padded chair behind his desk.

"What can I do for you, Reverend?" he asked, retrieving his whisky bottle from the desk drawer.

"I saw the new Stranger leave here a few minutes back. May I ask what you and he talked of?"

The Sheriff smiled at his visitor. "This particular Stranger is the one I mentioned a few days ago. He's the one hunting the Ivory Gang."

"I see. What did you tell him?"

"Just what Hook wanted: told him they'd more'n likely be holed up in the old Convent and he fell for it. Wouldn't be surprised to see him ride out any minute now."

The Reverend scowled at the fat man opposite him. "I still do not agree with your having truck with the Strangers, Sheriff, particularly those of Hook's ilk."

"Hell, Reverend, I just want to keep them out of Anchorhead is all. If this kid had approached me first then I'd have struck a deal with him and led Hook into an ambush." He looked over at the holy man and sipped at his whisky. "Besides, figured you to tar them all with the same brush. Seems a bit odd you saying some are worse than others," From the back room came the sound of a door opening then closing, causing all three men to glance in the direction. "My secretary," the Sheriff said with a leer, rubbing his crotch. The Reverend stood abruptly catching both his manservant and the Sheriff by surprise.

"As I said, Sheriff, my objection still stands and when Marshall Connor arrives I shall lodge my complaint with her. Good day to you." He turned and walked out. William nodded to the Sheriff then followed his master.

"Shit," the Sheriff muttered under his breath, reaching again for the whisky bottle. "Emma!" he shouted over his shoulder.

"You're late. Get your ass in here and do some work before I have to take my hand to you!" He poured a large glass for himself and knocked it back in one, topping it up almost immediately. "Emma! You get in here now or it ain't just gonna be my hand!"

"Seems too good to be true," Slake said, pulling his long dark coat on.

"What, you think it's a trap?" Justice said. "That Sheriff's too dumb to think of anything past his next glass of whisky."

"Yeah, but Hook isn't," Justice stopped at the back door of the Station and turned to the older Stranger.

"You think he could have put the Sheriff up to it?"

Slake shrugged. "It's possible. I haven't seen Hook for years, not since Kingston, but he was always a clever son of a bitch. I doubt he's changed much."

"So what do we do?" Dale asked.

"We go with what the kid says. Head off into the Maiden Hills and look for this abandoned Convent," Slake followed Justice out into the morning sun and across the road to the stables behind the Station, Dale catching them up as he buckled on his gun belt and holster.

"So you mean we could ride into a trap?" he asked.

"It's possible," Slake said with another shrug. "But then Hook and the others could be waiting in the stables right now, ready to blow our heads off as soon as we walk through the door."

"Now there's a comforting thought," Dale said, jamming his hat on his head.

From the doorway of his office, Sheriff Tidyman watched the three riders trot their horses out from behind the Station and head up the Main Street for the North gate. He was a little surprised to see the kid with two other Strangers, but figured the Ivory Gang could handle three as easily as one. With a sigh, he finished his glass of whisky and sauntered back inside, hollering for his secretary who still hadn't shown up; he'd heard her leaving, not entering.

Further along the street, the Reverend stood on the steps of the Church of Judas and watched the three Strangers ride out of town. He disapproved of Sheriff Tidyman's methods, but at least the Land would be rid of a few more Strangers at the end of this little episode. And, once he informed Marshall Connor, Anchorhead would almost certainly be rid of the inept lawman who freely consorted with known criminals.

At the North gate, the militia man gladly passed them through, spitting after them. He cursed them in the name of the true Christ whom the Reverend Diver claimed had been a Native betrayed by a Stranger and not the other way round.

"Anchorhead's a really nice place, kid," Dale said. "I'm glad I came along."

"You expect the Ivory Gang to hang out in a field of daisies?" Justice asked tight–lipped. "They're scum and that's what they hang around with."

"A word of advice, kid," Slake said quietly, lighting a jay. "Don't go into this thing all hot–headed. These people, as we all know, are killers. Keep cool. Don't get angry. If we can talk them into allowing you to settle your score with Hook then we will. If we can't, we'll just have to see what they do."

"You talk as if you've done this before."

Slake shrugged. "Once or twice."

They rode on in silence, following the dusty trail North. As they neared the hills, Slake and Dale relaxed in their saddles, watching Justice nervously fidgeting, checking and rechecking his pistol was loose enough in its holster.

"Who's that?" Dale asked, pointing ahead. Before them, waiting patiently in the road, was another horse and rider. As they drew closer, they could see it was a young woman wearing jeans, a blue work shirt with a tan leather waistcoat, a wide–brimmed hat and two pistols, one resting on each hip.

"Howdy, Strangers," she said as they drew up to her. "Which

one of you is the one after Hook?" The Strangers looked at each other, then Justice spoke up. "If you carry on any further up this road you're going to run straight into a trap. The Sheriff has sold you out to Hook and his friends. The Ivory Gang are waiting around the first bend after you get into the hills."

"How do you know?" Slake asked.

"My name's Emma. I'm the Sheriff's secretary, and I've been waiting for a chance to get even with that son of a bitch. And Hook."

"What the Hell are you on about?" Dale asked. "You appear from nowhere telling us we're riding into a trap, and now you're talking about some grudge against the Sheriff and Hook."

"The Ivory Gang are waiting for you just around from the main entrance into the hills. You ride in that way, you'll get killed. There's another, smaller route in from the side that'll bring you out right next to the Convent where you can wait for them or ride down and ambush their ambush, but you'll need me to show you where to go."

"And what do you want in return?" Slake asked.

"I want you to kill Sheriff Tidyman. And Hook," she said.

"This gets crazier every bloody minute," Dale said quietly to Slake. The four of them rode slowly up a rock strewn path, the three Strangers following Emma. "I swear I don't know what the Hell I'm doing here."

Slake grinned over at him. "You said yourself you weren't doing anything else at the moment. Who knows, you might even have a bit of fun."

"Yeah, or I might get my head blown off."

Emma brought her horse to a halt and waited while the others drew level.

"There you are: the Convent of Saint Mary."

The Strangers looked down the hill to the small white building in the centre of a miniature valley. It still bore the scars of the fighting it had seen during the Cynian–Aymian wars ten years before, weathered bullet holes dotted over its surface like the scars of an old disease. To the North lay the remains of a well, only the round wall having survived, and in the tower of the Convent a rusted bell still hung, though they could see no rope attached. The courtyard was bordered by a low wall that was mostly intact; a few boulders had rolled off the rocky hills, through the wall and into the yard.

"What a cheery place," Dale said.

"We'll leave the horses here," Slake said dismounting. "We'll need to be quiet. Chances are they've left someone on guard," the rest of them dismounted and tied the reins of their horses to the stump of a nearby tree. "If it's Hook, that'll make everything easier."

"And if it isn't?" Justice asked. Slake looked over at the young Stranger. All the colour had drained from his face and a sickly sweat trickled down his cheeks.

"We'll see what happens," Slake looked down the hill, pointing out the easiest way. As the three Strangers started down, Emma followed. "Where are you going?" Slake asked her.

"I've got guns and I know how to use them. Seems pointless my staying up here when you may need me."

"We're going down there to talk," Justice said.

Slake paused for a moment, then looked at Emma. "Come on."

As carefully and quietly as they could, the group headed down the tricky path, Dale muttering under his breath that he felt like a goat. As they neared the bottom, Slake held up his hand and crouched down as low as he could, the others immediately following suit.

The door of the Convent had opened, revealing a short man in jeans and a black jacket. They watched him walk around to the side away from them, passing out of sight behind the corner.

"Chain," Dale whispered.

"I'd be willing to bet he's taking a piss. Kid, get down there in plain sight and stay clear of the door."

"What?"

"Dale and Emma, circle around the other side so that you're almost opposite me. Make sure Chain doesn't see you as you go behind the Convent. Wait for my signal."

"So you get to stay here? Great," Dale said before jogging down the rest of the path and across the open space to the rear of the Convent, Emma following close behind.

"What are you doing Slake?" Justice asked.

"Just get down there and trust me," Slake said, looking at the scared kid. "Don't try and pull a gun on him, either. Wait for us."

Justice stared hard at him, his mouth suddenly dry, then walked quickly down the path and into the remains of the forecourt, the high sun casting a small shadow behind him. As he drew level with the building, Chain stepped around the corner.

"Don't shoot!" Justice said quickly, holding his hands out.

Chain leisurely drew a pistol from beneath his jacket, a smooth silver piece that glinted in the sunlight, completely different from Justice's standard revolver.

"Who are you?" he asked in a quiet tone of voice, his eyes squinting at Justice, the pistol never wavering.

"My name's Justice. I'm here to see Hook."

Slowly, Chain smiled, his few bad teeth jutting up from his gums.

"Take your gun out, slowly. Drop it on the floor," Justice did as he was told, removing his pistol, listening to it thud on the hard packed ground. "In the Convent."

Without taking his gaze from Chain's face, Justice began to move toward the dark interior of the building. Chain turned to watch him go, his pistol still levelled at him.

"Hook's been waiting for you to turn up," Chain said before his head exploded in a red haze. His body was thrown first to the left, then to the right as he was caught in the crossfire of Slake, Dale and Emma. His body fell to the floor, twitched once, then lay still.

Justice stared at the corpse before walking slowly over to his pistol and holstering it. The others strolled over, all three automatically replacing their spent bullets.

"One down," Dale said, looking at the ruined body. "What now?" he asked Slake.

"If the others are still waiting for us to come down the main road, I guess they'll have two on one side, one on the other. Try to catch us in a crossfire," Slake smiled ruefully, looking at Chain's body. "So if we went to get them, we'd have to split up."

"Or we could wait here," Emma said.

"That's probably our best move. We'd better move our dead friend here, before he leaves too much blood on the ground for us to cover up," Dale and Slake reached down and grabbed an arm and a leg each. They lifted the corpse and carried it around the side of the building. Emma walked into the Convent, leaving Justice to stare at the small dark pool of blood that had leaked out of Chain and stained the bare earth. There was a faint splash from the rear of the Convent and a moment later Dale and Slake reappeared.

"You okay, kid?" Slake asked him.

"I thought we were going to talk?" Justice said slowly, turning his head to look at him.

Slake shrugged. "Somehow, I don't think Chain was the talking kind. Chances are he'd have taken you in there and, if you were lucky, knocked you out to wait for his friends. If you were unlucky, torture's probably the least thing he'd have done to you." He placed his hand on Justice's shoulder. "Don't waste your grief mourning him, kid. The bastard's better off dead and down that well."

"Come on, kid," Dale said. "Let's see if they left anything we can get cooked up."

"I thought we were going to talk?" Justice said again.

"You don't talk with Strangers like these," Slake said, and walked into the Convent.

The interior of the Convent was made up mostly by one room which had served as both dining hall and church to the long gone nuns of Saint Mary, and it bore the same war torn markings as the exterior. There was no furniture, although Dale did find a small selection of pots in the Ivory Gang's packs which he then used to cook up some of the food they had left. Justice stood near one of the windows, keeping a nervous look out for the return of the rest of the gang, while Slake and Emma sat on the floor and talked.

"Can't say I like the idea of killing a Sheriff much," Slake said, examining one of the two pistols he had taken from Chain's body.

"Well I don't much like the idea of being groped and molested every time he's had too much to drink. Sooner or later the son of a bitch is going to go too far and try and rape me," Emma said. "It's hard to report that kind of thing when it's the Sheriff doing it."

"What's your problem with Hook?" he said in a quieter voice, glancing over to see whether Justice had heard them.

"The Sheriff threw me over to Hook as a way of keeping him sweet, so he would leave Anchorhead before him and his Gang tore the place up. I figure I owe both of them."

Slake sighed. "A deal's a deal. When we get back to Anchorhead –"

"If we get back," Dale said from the fireplace where he stirred the stew he had put together.

"Whoever gets back," Slake continued, "will sort out your Sheriff. Hopefully, we'll be able to sort out Hook here, one way or the other."

"If the kid there clears up his problem with Hook," Emma said, "I'm still going to take a shot at the bastard."

Slake looked at her for a second, then turned to Dale. "You ever seen one of these? I can't work the damn thing out," he said, sliding over Chain's second pistol. Dale picked it up and looked at the gun, so different from the revolvers they all used. At the press of a button, a cartridge, loaded with bullets, was ejected from the hand grip. Slamming it back in, Dale chambered a round by sliding the top half of the barrel back, then forward.

"Yeah," he said with a grin at Slake. "I've seen these. Stranger out near the Funeral Wastes had a few, a year or two back. I wanted one, but the price he was asking was way too high. You don't mind if I keep this one, do you?" he said, pocketing the pistol and stirring the stew again.

"Slake," Justice said from the window. "I see something."

Instantly Slake was at his shoulder, peering out of the window. In the distance three figures walked along the road leading to the Convent, a small, slight woman on the left, a man, the tallest of the three on the right, and another man in the middle.

"Well, well, if it isn't your friend and mine," Slake said. "How do you want to play this, kid?"

Justice stared at the figure of Hook as he approached. It had been seven years since he had last seen him, years of wandering the Land as a Stranger, searching for him. He remembered the words of the old woman who lived on the outskirts of Penny's Forest, remembered her telling him that all quests led to damnation. Or boredom. He had no doubt which he was facing here.

"Kid?" Slake asked. Behind the pair of them, Dale and Emma stood, both having checked their weapons, ready and waiting.

"I have to talk to Hook," Justice said.

"You're a fool, kid," Slake said, not unkindly. "He'll kill you as soon as he sees you."

"I have to talk to him. He knows where my parents are."

Slake sighed. "Alright. If he asks if anyone's with you, tell him you're on your own. If he asks about Chain, say you don't know him."

As Justice headed for the door, Slake called to Dale and Emma, telling them to take up positions at the window on the other side of the door. "Any shooting starts, Dale shoots at Ivory, Emma you take Hook and I'll have Rune," the pair nodded and stood at either side of the window.

"Best of luck, kid," Slake said as Justice reached for the door handle. He looked back at him and nodded, opened the door

95

and stepped out into the sunshine, waiting for the Ivory Gang.

They stepped over the remains of the low wall that bordered the courtyard, grinning at each other as they noticed Justice.

"Well, looky here," Hook said with a grin, pushing back the brim of his hat and staring at Justice. "Finally caught up with me then, Jimmy?"

"You told me to come and find you if I wanted to know where my parents were," Justice said. "Here I am."

Now that he stood before him, he had no idea what to do except move with the flow of things, to take his lead from Hook. If the Stranger wanted to talk, then Justice would talk. If he wanted to fight, Justice would be ready for him.

"This the little fuck you told me about?" Ivory said to Hook. Justice half hoped that Slake would shoot her now, take her out of the scene the way that Chain had been removed. She was the wildest of the three, completely unpredictable.

"Yeah," Hook said, still grinning at Justice, the teeth that had been smashed during their fight in Kingston now healed or replaced somehow. His hair had grown long and turned completely white. "This here's Jimmy, everybody. Jimmy, the Gang. Been trailing me for a few years now, huh?"

"Where the Hell is Chain?" Rune asked looking around the place, then at Justice.

"Who's Chain?" Justice asked steadily.

"That's real funny," Ivory said drawing her pistol in the time it took Justice to blink. "Where the fuck is he?"

"Listen," Justice said, holding his hands out. Things were moving too fast, the flow had turned into a torrent when he hadn't been looking. "I don't know this Chain. I just want to talk to Hook. Sort a few things out."

"What's to talk about, Jimmy?" Hook said. "You said you want to know where your parents are? Hell, kid, I'll be damned if I know. You wanting them so bad, I could see that blazing in your mind and took it to buy me some time. It was a delaying tactic, that's all it ever was. I just needed to mess you up long

96

enough so I could pull together about the only useful magic trick I ever knew which was disappearing in front of your eyes. I've never had the slightest idea where your parents are, and sure as Hell didn't expect you to spend this long chasing after me. You should have stayed at home."

He drew, Justice watching as if he were frozen as Hook pulled his pistol from his holster. He didn't bother extending his arm, but loosed off four shots from his hip, each one catching Justice in the chest, sending up great gouts of blood, pushing him backwards, off his feet, launching him momentarily into the air before he landed on his back in the dust and lay still.

Gunfire erupted from the Convent, bullets catching Hook in the gut and dropping him to the floor. Rune yelled as Slake's shot cut through his shoulder. He dived right, trying to hide as much of his tall frame as he could behind the few boulders. Ivory threw herself flat and scuttled off to the side, trying to lose herself in the sparse rubble, shouting and screaming obscenities at whoever was in the Convent. Hook lay on his back, a hand covering the holes in his stomach, feeling his life draining away moment by moment.

"Who the fuck is in that fucking thing?" Ivory screamed as the flat echoes of gunshots faded. For an answer a bullet punched through the undergrowth and threw up a cloud of dirt and pebbles as it hit the ground to her right.

"Looks like Jimmy . . . brought some . . . friends along," Hook gasped.

"You dumb fuck!" Ivory hissed, lowering her voice. She looked over to where Rune sat, a pistol in each hand, blood staining the brown leather coat he wore. He saw her and nodded. She turned back to Hook. "You're a fucking wizard! Do something!"

"In this state?" he whispered, holding his bloodied hand up.

"Throw down your weapons and stand with your hands in the air!" Slake shouted from the Convent.

"Hook, for fuck's sake do something!"

97

He coughed once, wincing at the pain in his stomach. He closed his eyes and concentrated for a moment. Ivory and Rune glanced at each other. With a cry, Hook reached out to the Convent, grinning as a sheet of flame sprung up from the ground in front of the windows.

Instantly, Ivory and Rune were up, shooting madly into the fire as they ran backwards as fast as they could, ducking down when someone shot from the Convent. As their bullets ran out, they turned and ran.

"I can't see a goddam thing!" Dale yelled, his hand in front of his eyes. He fired a couple of times out of the window, the flames hiding any targets. Less than half a minute later and, as quickly as they had appeared, the flames were gone.

The three ducked out of sight, Slake and Emma trying to look out into the forecourt.

"Can you see anything?" Emma asked.

"I still got bloody stars in front of my eyes," Dale moaned, rubbing at them.

"I can't see anyone except Hook and the kid," Slake said, peering out his window.

"I hate these damn situations," Dale said. "You think they're all dead, you go out to check them and up pops one bastard and bang! You're dead instead of them." He blinked, his vision returning slowly.

"What do we do?" Emma asked. She waved away the residue of the gun smoke from the window and carefully looked out. Two bodies lay on the ground in front of her when there should have been four. Slake's first shot had hit Rune, but Dale had missed Ivory. They were either hiding somewhere out there or had ran off. "I agree," she said. "I hate these situations too."

"I can't see her," Dale said. "Mind you, I can't see much."

"Wish I knew more about her," Slake said. "Maybe have an idea of how she works."

"I think she's pretty much a hit and run type. Least I hope

so."

"Emma, check if there's a rear exit to this place," Slake looked out at Justice's fallen body, a widening pool of blood spreading out beneath it. He sighed and shook his head, trying to dodge the feelings of guilt that were even now attempting to make their way into his head.

"We're in luck," Emma said from the back of the room. "There's a back door and a stairway up to the next floor and I think it goes up to the bell tower as well."

"Okay," Slake stood and thought for a moment, rubbing at the stubble on his chin. "Quick as you can, get up to the tower and have a look around, see if you can find Ivory's hiding place. If you see her or Rune and can get a clear shot, feel free."

She disappeared again, leaving Slake and Dale to stand and wait near the windows, neither of them able to take their gaze from the carnage in the courtyard of the Convent. As they waited the long minutes before Emma returned, the first flies of the afternoon descended upon the bodies.

Slake turned to face Emma as she walked back through the main room.

"Not a sign of either of them."

"They don't know how many of us there are in here," Slake mused, almost to himself. "If Ivory's got any sense, she'll head off."

"If she has any sense," Dale said.

"Well, we've gotta move sometime," Slake said and opened the door, stepping out into the still afternoon air, pistols ready. Despite himself, he found he had held his breath passing through the doorway as if by leaving the cool gloom of the Convent and entering the dry heat of the courtyard he had plunged into a river, nervous of the unknown dangers that lay within. He walked slowly over to Justice's body, allowing Ivory or Rune plenty of time in which to shoot him if they were still around, though they could have been waiting for everyone to leave the Convent and pick them all off. Looking over at the bushes in which Ivory had hidden herself, he knelt beside the young Stranger, brushing aside the small cloud of flies he disturbed.

"Dumb kid," he said quietly, unbuckling Justice's gun belt and pulling it off him. "Didn't even get to practice what Exit taught you," Slake hung the belt over his shoulder and moved over to Hook stopping when he found him smiling up at him.

"Slake? That you?" he asked quietly. Slake knelt at his side, but not without first noticing Hook's pistol lay beyond reach.

"Yeah, it's me."

"Shit . . . Funny . . . how it all . . . turns out . . . don't you think?"

"What do you mean, Hook?"

He grinned slightly. "Pair of us . . . out at Kingston . . . now we're . . . both here . . . Funny, huh?" Slake nodded. "Any idea . . . . what happens . . . now? Do you . . . do you think . . . we go back?"

Before Slake could answer, Hook coughed, throwing up blood over his chin. He sighed, the sound bubbling up from his throat, then was silent. Slake remained there for a moment, then unbuckled Hook's gun belt and pulled it out from under him. He walked back to Dale and Emma.

"Come on, let's get out of here."

"He dead?" Emma asked, pointing at Hook. Slake nodded. "Good."

They rode quietly and slowly back to Anchorhead, leaving the fallen where they lay, to the flies, buzzards and wolves. By the time they reached the North gate, the militia had already locked up and were reluctant to open.

"Sorry, no Strangers allowed in after the gates are locked," the militia man said.

"What about Natives?" Emma said, nudging her horse forward.

"Emma? That you?"

"'Course it's me. It can't be later than noon. What are you

100

doing closing the gates at this time? Open them."

"Can't do it. Reverend Diver's orders." The militia man looked up at her. "What you doing riding with a couple of Strangers anyhow?"

"Sheriff's business," she replied smoothly, "and since when does some visiting Preacher run the militia?"

"Since Sheriff Tidyman told us to obey his orders," he hung his head and shook it slowly. "Sheriff's been in a foul mood since this morning, Emma. We heard it was because you'd gone off unexpected. He's been drunk all day."

"Is that anything unusual?" Emma said. "Open the gate, Frank." He stood looking at her for a minute or so then sighed, reached out to the big wooden bar and lifted it up, easing the gate open to allow all three riders to trot inside.

"Are you sure this is what you want Emma?" Slake asked as they rode along, ignoring the stares of the few people on the streets. "You know what'll happen? You've been seen with us now. There's no going back once that trigger is pulled."

"I know."

As they neared the Sheriff's office, they saw a large group of people gathered in front of the Station. They all listened to the ranting of the Reverend Diver who stood on the Station's porch, as he had the evening before when he had overseen the hanging of the Stranger named Canyon.

"These Strangers are an abomination in the eyes of the Lord!" he shouted, waving his copy of the Book in his hand. "No longer should Anchorhead or any of the towns in the Mainland Kingdoms play host to the defilers of our Lands! With your help brothers and sisters, we can purge the Kingdoms of this foul breed, push them Westward into the Funeral Wastes where they may lie and rut with the hairy beasts of that Land!"

"Judas, he goes on," Dale said.

"Is there a back way into the Sheriff's office, Emma?" Slake nodded down towards the group watching the Preacher. "If we try and ride past them we'll be torn to pieces."

"Follow me," she said. They turned off the main street and rode down a small alley that ran between the back gardens of two streets. Even on the other side of the houses the shouting of the Preacher could still be heard, spurting out his bigoted views for the easily led masses. As they drew level with the Sheriff's office, Slake dismounted and checked his pistol.

"Slake?" Emma said. He looked up at her. "None of you asked for any proof from me. There's no reason for you to believe me. You haven't even asked why I haven't shot him myself."

"I know. But you saved our lives back there. We would have ridden into an ambush." He shrugged. "A deal's a deal. I ain't too worried about the right and wrong of it." He nodded at her, walked up the path to the back door and opened it. Emma looked over at Dale who shrugged and looked back at the Sheriff's office. They sat in silence for a few moments, half listening to the ravings of the Reverend on the other side of the building, then both sat up as two shots were fired. As Slake walked out of the back door, Dale said "They've gone awful quiet over there."

"Come on," Slake said, mounting his horse. "Let's get out of here."

"The South gate's the nearest," Emma said.

It took them mere minutes to reach it, only to find it locked and guarded by more of the militia. As the Strangers sat on their horses arguing with the guards to let them out, the mob that had moved from the Station to the Sheriff's office seemed to turn as one huge beast, possessed of a single mind, an intelligence that belonged to just one of their number who directed their actions with his words.

"There are the Strangers!" the Reverend shouted. "There stand the killers of your Sheriff, the defilers of your town!" The crowd roared its anger and surged toward them.

"If you don't want to get shot by us or crushed by them," Slake said to the militia men, "open that bloody gate!" As the men wavered, nervously staring at the fast approaching crowd, Dale jumped down from his saddle and pushed them aside, lifted the large bar that locked the gate and swung it wide. The crowd shrieked, fearful of being cheated of their righteous fury and seemed to put on speed. Dale swung up on his horse and the three rode out, the mob swarming behind them, screaming their rage as the horses kicked dirt and dust up into their faces. Beyond the limits of the town, however, as the Strangers out ran them, the crowd were less willing to continue the chase and milled around the gate instead, calling and gesturing to the horse riders.

"Strangers!" came the Reverend's voice.

Safe now from the mob, the three riders paused and turned around, watching the small man walk forward, separating himself from the crowd that hushed itself as its leader spoke with a quiet strength.

"Strangers, know that you cannot escape, neither the law of this Land, nor the just and true fury of our Lord Judas. The legal power of the Mainland Kingdoms will be sent after you, and the divine wrath of Christ will descend upon you. We will seek you out, wherever you may hide your heathen forms. There will be no haven for you or your kind. You will be sought after. You will be hunted."

Dale drew the pistol he had taken from Rune and aimed at the Reverend who stood, unflinching.

"Leave it," Slake said. "You'd only make him a martyr."

Reluctantly, Dale holstered his pistol. They stared at the Reverend and the mob behind him, then turned their horses to the South.

"There's bound to be a posse after us, not to mention Ivory and Rune," Dale said, chewing on the salted ham from his pack. "The preacher was right: we're going to be hunted."

"Wouldn't be the first time," Slake said with a smile.

"Speak for yourself," Emma said. They chuckled together, sat around their campfire, looking up at the stars and moons above them.

"Where do you figure on going?" Dale asked eventually.

Slake shrugged. "I'm not sure. Out of the Mainland Kingdoms, I know that. I wondered about the Sadducee Plains. There's a couple of Walkers up there I know, but . . . I don't know. I haven't long left them," He fell silent for a moment. "Guess I'll head West, towards the Funeral Wastes. Maybe visit one of the towns around there."

"Well, I ain't doing anything else right now. Mind if I come along?" Slake smiled over at him.

"What about you, Emma?" he said. "You fancy riding with known outlaws?"

"Would that make me a Stranger?" she asked them.

Slake shrugged. "Near as damn it. Near as Justice was, anyhow."

Emma sat and thought for a moment. "You never asked me for any proof, Slake," she said. "Proof why I wanted the Sheriff dead."

He shrugged. "I told you earlier, I owed you. You saved us from walking into an ambush."

"And it's as simple as that, is it? As black and white as a checker board?"

"That's how I work, how my life runs."

She scratched idly in the dirt, sifting through the small pebbles, tossing the larger ones to one side.

"For years, he got drunk and pawed at me no matter how many times I knocked him down and hit him. He'd have his hands inside my dress as often as they were wrapped round a bottle. A Season back, the son of a bitch actually went so far as to walk in on me when I was in the bathroom; had his trousers round his ankles and his dander up," she smiled with no humour at all. "A quick punch put an end to that idea, at least for that day.

"Then Hook came along and I got thrown to him to keep him sweet. He arrived a few days before the rest of his gang, otherwise I guess the others would have had their fun, too," Emma looked at them both. "After that, I figured enough was enough. You guys coming along gave me the perfect chance to stop being Emma Tidyman."

"Tidyman? But the Sheriff's name . . . ?" Dale said.

Emma nodded, her eyes free of tears. "That fat, drunken bastard was my uncle."

They sat in silence for some time, staring at the campfire.

"I'll need a name, won't I? If I'm going to be a Stranger?" She asked.

"Let's think about that in the morning. We all need to get some sleep; it's a hell of a ways to the Funeral Wastes," Slake said.

They set about getting their bedrolls ready, laying in a triangle around the fire, each of them facing towards it.

"You think Justice got what he wanted?" Emma asked. "When he was speaking to Hook, I mean."

"I doubt it," Slake said. "We hardly ever get that in life. Doesn't matter if you're Native, Stranger, Clansman, Walker or whatever the hell else. All you get is what you're given."

"Slake? How's about you give us some peace so we can get to sleep?" Dale said.

He pulled his blanket up to his chin and closed his eyes.

By the time the posse found the remains of the camp the next morning, the Strangers were gone. The townsfolk who owned horses were reluctant to chase after them, despite the exhortations of the good Reverend. The land to the South and West, as they pointed out, soon changed from scrubland to rocky foothills; the chances of following their tracks through that were slim.

Slowly, they began to drift back to Anchorhead until only the Reverend and his manservant William were left.

"What happens now, sir?" the boy asked quietly.

Reverend Diver sighed, staring out across the foothills, his manservant behind him.

"These things never end, William. Sooner or later, those Strangers will be found, either by the law or the Lord. They will not go unpunished, though we may not be involved; they will not live forever, though we may not be the cause of their deaths; and at some point we may learn their fate, though we may never see them again.

"That is the way of the Land, my boy: we see only glimpses of the lives of others, as though we look through a window and they pass in front of us. Sometimes that makes us content, sometimes it is best not to know what happens once they leave our view. At other times it is an irritation, one that we must learn to live with. Either way, it is the end, for now."

He turned to where William waited and stopped short. The young man was gone, replaced with a tall man dressed in breeches and a jacket made up of mismatched patches of cloth coloured red and green. On his head he wore a hat with three points, one to either side of his head, the other reaching up before drooping to his right; each point was topped with a small silver bell. His face was lit up by a huge grin and his eyes sparkled.

"Reverend Diver," he said, bowing low before the stunned preacher and then standing upright again. "It is my very great pleasure to meet you, sir."

"Who . . . who in the name of Judas are you?" the Reverend asked, taking a step or two backwards. "Where is William?"

"I'm sorry, Reverend, but he was in the way," the jester said, pointing at his feet. He stood upon a pile of clothes that the Reverend recognised as William's. They were flattened and already stained a deep, rich red by the blood that flowed from within. "You and I, however, need to have a little conversation."

He jumped towards the Reverend, the bells on his hat ringing, his grin widening, his teeth shining.

If anyone from the posse heard the Reverend's scream, they did not turn or stop.

STILL WATERS

Marshall Connor pulled on her large duster coat and buttoned it up, then jammed her hat on to her head and yanked the strap tight under her chin. The weather outside had been getting steadily worse for several days, the cold Season's last snap. Snow sat atop the hills to the North of Jerusalem though there seemed to be less each day. The wind refused to die, however, screaming in at night across the plains to the West, carrying with it the stench of the distant Funeral Wastes. It had been one of the coldest Seasons in history, according to the old timers, but Connor seemed to hear that every year.

With her gloves on, she opened the door to her room and walked out into the corridor. She passed only one other person in the hotel on her way to the stairs, a young man with his first attempt at a moustache bravely clinging to his top lip. They nodded at each other but didn't speak; the eight pointed star she wore on her coat seemed to strike most civilians dumb, a reaction she was used to. She waved to the girl at the reception desk when she reached the bottom of the stairs, then opened the door and walked out.

The King's End Road was busy even this early in the morning with people starting their day, moving from place to place. Riders on horseback, as well as a few carriages, went to and fro along the road that, with the night's rain and early morning frost, was already a quagmire. The smells of cooking, horse dung and the damp earth were almost swamped by the cloying scent of the nearby paper mill. It was the largest of the two in the Mainland Kingdoms and went some way to accounting for Jerusalem's wealth, but it stank.

As Connor walked along the raised wooden walk ways that ran along the sides of the road, she found herself wondering – and not for the first time – why the overwhelming sensation of living in the capital was of bad smells. She tugged her scarf up out of the collar of her coat and covered her mouth and nose, only partly due to the cold.

The city had been founded hundreds of years before, by Judan settlers travelling Westward from the Frontiers. Named after the mythical city beyond the Eastern mountains where Judas had supposedly lived and preached, Jerusalem grew from a motley collection of huts into a hamlet, buoyed by the farmers that were attracted by the fertile lands around it. Travellers began stopping off at the site which began catering to them, turning it into a town. Merchants and mercenaries stationed themselves there which increased the security of the Natives, drawing more and more settlers to the town which soon became a city. In the turbulent years which resulted in the foundation of the Mainland Kingdoms, Jerusalem became the focus of the negotiations to end the wars and, when the last treaty was signed, the city became the capital.

Throughout its existence, Jerusalem had evolved from a purely Judan site to one which embraced all faiths. It had been said that for every road there was a church, a statement that was only a slight exaggeration. Buildings for the worship of Judas Christ were sometimes across from a church dedicated to the Cuckoo God; two streets away from that was an open grass area sacred to the Land Lord; around the corner was a multi-columned temple to the many gods of the Ancient Elders. Worshippers of these and other faiths lived, traded, loved and died together, bound by the laws of the city that rejected religious intolerance.

108

Connor walked past a temple of R'lyeh, its stonework decorated with octopus headed figures that, in the dull morning light filtered through the mist, seemed to writhe and move. One of the temple's priests stood at the top of the steps that led up to the doorway, the shoulders of his robes decorated with the same types of figures, their bejewelled eyes staring at the world.

"He comes, Marshall!" he called out. "The enemy of the world makes his move as we sleep and even great R'lyeh trembles before his foot falls!"

She raised her hand and waved at him, walking past. The preachers of R'lyeh were renowned doom criers and some people travelled to Jerusalem just to see them.

"He comes for us all, Marshall!" the preacher cried after her.

It took her about fifteen minutes to reach her destination: the Halls of Justice. It was a large building, one of the many made primarily from stone rather than wood. The Halls housed the heart of the Mainland Kingdoms' judiciary and law enforcers; the law books, two large tomes containing the laws of the Land, were constantly on display behind glass cases protected by armed guards and, supposedly, magical wards. The Marshals of the Land were based here also and, after years of almost constant travelling, it was the closest thing Connor had to a home.

She walked up the two dozen steps to the main entrance, nodding to one or two other Marshals as they came and went. Inside, she pulled her scarf down from her face and smiled at the older woman behind the main desk.

"Samantha!" the woman exclaimed, coming out from behind the desk and hugging the Marshall. "My word, girl, it's been so long since you've been in town."

"Hello, Julia," Connor replied. They stepped back and looked at each other, both of them noticing the signs of age on the other, neither of them caring. "How have you been?"

"Not too bad at all, dear," Julia said. "Things have been pretty quiet all round for the most part. Your father's been bored out of his mind."

"Is he in yet?"

"Oh yes, you know him," she glanced up at the clock on the wall. "If you're lucky, you might catch him before he heads off for his coffee."

"He's still in the same office?"

"Yes, dear. Up the stairs, second on the right."

Connor hugged her again.

"It's so good to see you, Julia. We'll have a good catch up later, okay?"

"Count on it. Now go see your father."

Connor took the stairs, pulling off her gloves and unbuttoning her coat as she did so. The corridor was lit by a handful of paraffin wax lamps that gave off a dull yellow glow that helped the sparse morning light that filtered through the window at the end. Several doors led off from the corridor and she tapped at the one with the plaque that read "Chief Marshall Frank Connor."

"Come in," the voice was deep and more than a little irritated; Connor knew her father wasn't at his best this early in the day.

She opened the door and walked in, stepping across the room until she stood in front of his desk. Her father sat behind it, reading some papers, annotating them now and then.

"What do you – Samantha!" His gruff tone softened as he looked up at her, instantly standing and going to greet her with a hug and a peck on the cheek. "I didn't think you'd be in town for another couple of weeks?"

"I managed to get one of my cases finished earlier than I was expecting." They commented on each others' appearances, Connor complaining she was too thin, her father saying he was too fat. "Have you had your coffee yet?" she asked.

"I was going to head down and get some any time now," Frank said.

"Then let me buy you one."

They made their way to the food hall in the basement of the building where everyone who worked there – Marshals, Judges, secretaries or janitors – ate at some time. It was plain and straightforward, much like the food on offer, but was a damn sight cheaper than anywhere else in the city.

The pair of them bought some coffee with Connor getting some toast as well.

"How's mum?"

"She's doing okay. Julia and I saw her a week or two ago; we went to see your step-brother in one of his plays," Frank pulled a face.

"You in a theatre? Things have changed," Connor said with a smile. Her parents had divorced many years ago and, while it had been tricky at first, they'd each moved on and married again, her father to Julia, the head receptionist. Her mother had married an accountant, a widower with a son a year or two younger than Connor. She'd been to one or two of her step-brother's plays where he both acted and directed and, like her father, found them to be almost incomprehensible.

They talked about what they'd been doing in work, swapping stories and comparing notes, Frank occasionally offering advice. Connor had become a Marshall thanks to Frank's parenting – he encouraged her to find her own interests and work out what she wanted to do herself. Time and again she came back to being a King's Marshall until both he and her mother agreed and put her into the School of Law. Even after Marshalling for over ten years, though, she was grateful for her father's advice.

"So what's coming up?" Connor asked, referring to the outstanding warrants that were a Marshall's bread and butter.

"Couple of odd ones which I thought might interest you, actually," Frank said. "There's a warrant on two Strangers and a Native from about three Seasons ago; they killed a Sheriff in Anchorhead off to the North East and no-one's seen them since. They're also suspected of having kidnapped a Preacher."

"Strangers and Natives killing together? That is odd."

"Or there's the town called Jonestown down South on the edge of the Blue States; seems a Stranger wandered in to it a few Seasons back and convinced most of the townsfolk to leave with him and go live with his god. Place is pretty much deserted by all accounts."

"That's happened before, hasn't it?"

"Sure has. Happening more and more often, too. It's the second time I've heard it in as many years."

"Anything else?"

"There's rumours of a Stranger organising hunting parties that go looking for game in the Funeral Wastes out West. People who've gone and never come back, that sort of thing."

"I'm surprised anyone actually falls for that these days."

Frank chuckled. "I know what you mean. Still, we've gotta look into it. There is one last one though it's probably a bit risky."

"Aren't they all, dad?" Connor knew her father well; he wasn't one to go for the drawn out pause and the dramatic sigh. If he thought this case was risky, he told her straight.

"The Ivory Gang have been up to their old tricks again, only this time they've pissed off the wrong people.

"About three Seasons back they came in from the North-East, skirted past Jerusalem and headed back up North. By all accounts they were one or two members short; we only had a definite sighting of Ivory and the big fella, Rune. We don't know where Chain, Hook or Hollow are. About three days ago, we had a report come in that Ivory and Rune were heading South just as fast as they can, not bothering to put too much distance between them and the city, neither. Two days after that, this was yesterday, we found out why. A dozen Clansmen are chasing them."

"Clansmen? This far South?"

"A-huh. Never seen nor heard it happen before, but those two idiot Strangers have pissed them off enough to chase them into the Mainland Kingdoms."

Connor and her father stared at each other before she asked "So what are we going to do about it?"

"Couple of Marshals are all set and ready to go. Course, we could use another to make up the numbers."

Connor sat back in her chair and looked around the canteen. Of the handful of Marshals that were in there, only herself and another looked older than thirty. Marshals tended not to live that long, the survivors coming here to the Halls of Justice to teach, serve as judges and while away their years. The younger Marshals were usually abroad in the Kingdoms, returning to Jerusalem when they had to. Either that or they were already dead.

"There don't seem to be many active Marshals here, dad. How many are you sending against the Clansmen?"

"I've got two others and, I'm sorry to say, one of them graduated three weeks ago."

"Sweet Judas," Connor sat in thought. "The other one?"

"John McKinley. Bit of a tough nut type, prefers working on his own but knows how to work with others when he has to. Plus he's part Clansmen himself which can't hurt."

Connor was nodding as he spoke.

"Yeah, I met him last year. Can be a bit standoffish and quiet, but he's a good man."

"You want the job? You'd be senior Marshall."

Connor smiled.

She swam offshore, in water that was only four feet deep but the shore was nowhere to be seen and she couldn't touch the sea floor when she stood. The waters, warm and clear when she had started swimming, were now cold and muddy. She felt things move against her legs as the bright blue sky darkened above her until it was indistinguishable from the ocean.

Her hair floated around her as she realised she had gone under, the silt heavy water obscuring her sight almost completely. Shadows that felt slimy wrapped themselves around her thin, scarred body and tugged her down even further.

Sound reached her water clogged ears, a rhythmic humming, at once melodic and yet broken. It grew louder as the shadows, their surfaces lined with teeth-laden suckers, latched on to her. She cried out, air bubbles escaping her mouth, each holding a scream within it.

The sound grew louder still, forming words of a long dead language that she could still understand.

"He comes. He comes. The Ruiner. The Enemy. He brings the End of the Land."

The shadow tentacles gripped tighter and she could feel the teeth of the suckers gnawing at her flesh. Smaller suckers inside them, mouths within mouths, bit into the fresh wounds, eating away at her.

A figure approached, pushing through the silt, somehow silhouetted against the depths as if it were darker than the abyss.

"The End of the Land. He comes. It ends. It will all end. Help me."

She screamed again, sending the last few bubbles fleeing to the surface as the figure became clear and mighty R'lyeh swam before her, his head a mass of tentacles at the base of a huge domed head dominated by a single, yellow eye that glowed from the darkness.

She screamed and the water took her breath away.

Connor avoided walking past the temple of R'lyeh the next morning. Though she held no belief in prophetic visions and the like, the dream had unnerved her. She saw no need to freshen the thankfully fading images by walking past the temple.

The night before, she and her extended family had watched her step-brother perform on stage. As her father had hinted, the play was long and boring, telling the story of a woman tasked with tutoring the many children of a widower and ultimately helping them escape from an invading army. Connor had sat through it, thinking of the many, many other things she would rather have been doing.

Following the play, she and her family went for a meal before she returned to her hotel. At some early hour of the morning, she had woken from her nightmare, covered in sweat, the image of R'lyeh still vivid in her mind's eye, his words ringing in her ears.

At the Halls of Justice, she met up with her father and the two Marshals she would be riding with in search of the Ivory Gang. John McKinley was as she remembered him; tall and rugged, his faced tanned after years of riding in the sun, he was polite but brief. He said little unless he had to and found it almost impossible to make small talk, a trait that had often earned him the description of arrogant. The other Marshall was just as Connor expected.

Three weeks out of the Academy, Daniel Blue-Wing was enthusiastic, eager and keen all rolled into one big ball of nervousness. He wanted to get going, to find the law breakers and bring them to justice. He was more than ready to fight, itching to draw his pistol in the course of the law.

Connor had to admit that when she'd left the Academy, she'd been much the same.

They spent the day preparing for a long trip, taking provisions for both themselves and their horses; while the countryside would provide their mounts with most of their needs, it didn't hurt to have some extras set aside. They made sure their pistols were clean and loaded and that they had extra ammunition; McKinley had a rifle strapped to his saddle as well.

By midday they were ready to go. Connor said goodbye to her father and Julia and asked them to pass on her best to her mother. Blue-Wing's parents came to see him off, the mother unashamedly crying as her little boy went off on his first adventure into the big, bad Land. McKinley had no-one to say farewell to and didn't seem particularly bothered by it.

They left Jerusalem with the noon sun riding high.

It took them two days before they found someone who had either seen the Ivory Gang or the Clansmen who were following them. A small shack in the middle of nowhere was home to an old, sun-dried woman who sat on the porch in a rocker, slicing apples with a small paring knife and popping the pieces into her toothless mouth. She squinted up at them as they drew near and waved amiably enough.

"I seen 'em," she said when Connor asked her about their quarry. "Headed out West they did, and a day or two later a large band of wild men came rushing through, chasing their sorry asses."

Connor wondered what state the Clansmen had to be in for the old woman to think of them as wild men.

"Headed West?" McKinley asked her. "Are you sure?"

"Sure as I'm sitting here, Marshall. Told them there was nothing out that way and that the nearest town was more than a week's ride South, but they headed West alright."

McKinley turned to Connor. "The Funeral Wastes butt on to the plains only a few miles away from here. Think they're headed out there?"

"Probably. Plenty of places to hide up and lose the Clansmen. Hell, from what little I know about them, the Clansmen might even give up rather than enter the Wastes."

"Why's that, Marshall?" Blue-Wing asked her.

"They're a superstitious lot by all accounts. No offence, John," she added to McKinley.

"None taken."

"The Wastes are supposedly haunted and they might not want to risk finding out for sure."

The woman watched them as they talked, her pale, sun-bleached eyes moving from one to the other as she ate her slices of apple.

"Well," Connor said after a moment's thought. "I guess we're heading West."

They thanked the old woman, turned their horses and rode off. As the sound of the hooves faded and their silhouettes began to blur with distance, she looked over her shoulder.

"You can come out now," she said.

The jester walked out of the hut, his clothes made up of mismatched red and green patches adding an unwanted splash of colour to the scrubland. The bells on his hat tinkled with each step he took as he reached the woman in her rocker.

"You didn't say it would take this long," she said with more than a hint of bitterness. "I've been waiting here for years."

"I did tell you it would be a long time," the jester said, making no apology. "But still, you've done your work for me now. Your debt is cleared."

The woman sighed and looked around her meagre home.

"I miss Penny's Forest. At least there things grew. Out here there's nothing but dust and death."

"Speaking of which," the jester said, taking hold of her head in both hands. She didn't have time to scream as he pulled, her spine cracking, the dry tendons in her throat snapping, the tough cartilage of her windpipe tearing as her head came away from her shoulders. Blood pumped weakly from the red stump until her heart realised she was dead.

The jester walked round to the fenced-in back yard of the hut and tossed the woman's head on to the mound of Clansmen, disturbing the flies that feasted on their bodies. Each of them had been killed by their own swords being driven through their bodies, staking them to the ground or each other.

"Can't have any loose ends," he said to himself.

While the soil of the plains was tough, grasses and a few other shrubs had managed to grow there. Where people had settled in small holdings, crops could be raised though it was hard work. Animals, grazing herds mostly, roamed the Land, walking constantly from one grassy plain to the next. They left the ground mostly bare except for their droppings which would aid the next generation of grasses to grow before the herds returned.

Nothing grew in the Funeral Wastes.

The edge of the Wastes was clear – a line of black rock broke up out of the ground with sharp, jagged edges. Dust and sand were blown into the Wastes but even that could not blur the definite distinction between the two. The farther West they went, the taller the rocks became. A few miles in, clear in the sunlight, jagged, spiked columns of rock rose up. They merged to form hills and eventually mountains in the distance, huge slabs of rock that were meant to be impassable.

Other than the first few miles, the Wastes were unmapped. Few people cared to enter them as there was nothing there unless you believed the tales of ghosts. Dead men and women were said to walk the few trails that led to the foothills; their cries and shrieks warned travellers away from the perils of the Wastes.

The Marshals had stopped at a small hamlet, the last before the Wastes. It was little more than a collection of a dozen or so huts, and they re-stocked their supplies as best they could. No-one there had seen either the Ivory Gang or the Clansmen and Connor had to consider the possibility of having lost their trail.

"The only fools heading into the Wastes are hunters up from the Blue States. Some Stranger named Saxon meets up with them a few miles out of town and leads them in. We don't see them again," the town's headman told her.

Connor had discussed with McKinley and Blue-Wing what to do. It seemed either the old woman had been wrong or had lied to them; either that or, somehow, they had lost the trail. The Stranger organising hunting parties, however, seemed to be nearby and as they were in the area, might be worth investigating.

"No offence, Connor, but one Stranger suckering hunters from down South doesn't warrant three Marshals," McKinley had said. "If we ain't heading out after Ivory and company, I don't see the need for us to remain together."

"Yeah, I know what you mean," Connor had said. "I heard about the hunting party thing before we left Jerusalem. Didn't want to get involved in it."

"So what do we do?" Blue-Wing asked.

"Ivory's either slipped past us or we've been diverted," Connor said. "John, you head South East, see if you can pick up the trail again. If you do, get word to us here. Meantime, young Daniel and I will look into this Stranger and his hunting scam. You've got to head into the Funeral Wastes at some point, son," she'd said to Blue-Wing. "May as well be sooner rather than later."

After McKinley had left, Connor spoke to the headman to get as much information about the Stranger as possible. Now, two days later, she and Blue-Wing sat on their horses at the edge of the Funeral Wastes.

"You think the Wastes really are haunted, Marshall?" Blue-Wing asked.

"I've seen some odd stuff over the years: Strangers using magic; people surviving gunshots that would kill a normal person; one woman who seemed to breathe underwater. One thing I've never seen, though, is a ghost."

She moved her horse forward, letting it pick its own way through the sharp rocks. The trail they were following was an accident of nature; at some point over the years, an eruption had taken place and a number of lava flows had wormed their way over the rock. The few travellers or explorers who had ventured into the Wastes had mapped the flows and the headman of the hamlet had given Connor a copy. It seemed likely that any supposed hunters would follow the trails into the Wastes in search of prey.

As far as Connor knew, there were no animals to hunt in the bleak landscape. It had no vegetation for animals to eat and what little water there was tended to be stagnant. The wind came from the West, beyond the mountains which, for the most part, prevented any clouds forming over the Wastes. Rainfall happened once every three or four years and was thin when it fell.

If a Stranger was leading people into this place, it seemed unlikely that they would be hunting anything other than each other.

They rode in silence, following the lava paths on their map, the ground rising as they went further West. They stopped occasionally to rest the horses and to eat some food but for the most part just kept going.

They camped at nightfall, building a fire with the wood they'd brought with them, and cooked a simple meal. The lava trail was the flattest surface available and they spent the night wrapped in bedrolls and blankets on the path.

Blue-Wing woke in the night to the sound of someone screaming, a high pitched wail that would drop off suddenly before starting again. Low moans sometimes accompanied it and in the pitch darkness he couldn't help thinking of ghosts walking the desolate land around him. He debated waking Connor but thought better of it; his first trip out as a Marshall shouldn't include a report on his childlike fear of noises in the dark.

When Connor woke in the morning, Blue-Wing was already up and had the fire going, coffee brewing on it.

Taking the coffee he offered her, she noticed the dark patches beneath his eyes.

"Did you sleep well?" she asked.

He shook his head and smiled a little.

"The sounds of the dead kept me awake."

"You realise it's probably just the wind blowing through the rocks, don't you?"

He nodded. "You realise it's the word 'probably' in your sentence that isn't comforting?"

Connor chuckled and drank her coffee.

By mid-morning they were off the edge of their map. The lava flow they'd been following ended at the base of a cliff. It had fallen from the top leaving lumpy stalactites across its face but, unless their horses could climb sheer cliffs, they had to find their own way forward.

"There's what looks like another flow a mile or so over that way," Blue-Wing said when Connor asked for his opinion. "It looks like it climbs the cliff as well."

Connor looked at it: it was steep and they'd probably have to walk their horses up it but it seemed passable. Getting to it across the sharp rocks, however, was another matter. The land between them and the path was made up of large boulders for the most part, too few of which formed any sort of surface suitable for the horses. Gaps between them could quickly lead to broken legs for either their horses or themselves.

"I'm not sure we can get the horses across," Connor said.

"We're going to have to leave them here, take what we can and make the best of it. Hopefully we'll come across the Stranger and his band of hunters sooner rather than later."

They unpacked their saddle bags and divided what they could into their backpacks. Leaving food for the horses, they made their way slowly across the rocks. It took them about two hours of climbing and crawling, sometimes literally, over the terrain to reach the path. Blue-Wing's estimation of a mile or so was a little bit of wishful thinking; it turned out to be closer to three, the twisted and blasted rocks deceptively altering the distance.

It was with a huge sense of relief that they climbed from the last boulder on to the smooth lava flow. They rested for a while, treating the few cuts and grazes they'd picked up on their journey. Their gloves had protected their hands for the most part, though they had both torn them.

Connor looked up the steep slope ahead.

"Ready for this?" she asked him.

"Not really," he said.

With a weary sigh from both of them, they shouldered their backpacks again and began to climb.

The incline quickly tired their legs; their thighs started to burn after a few dozen steps. Within a few minutes they were both breathing hard, their hands resting on their knees as they walked hunched over. Trying to straighten their backs became a chore as the backpacks weighed them down. There was no conversation on the climb; they didn't bother to look to their right across the desolate landscape; their concentration was fixed solely on placing one foot in front of another.

They stopped about half way up and took a drink but carried on as soon as their bottles were stoppered again. Anything more than the briefest of pauses made their legs seize up, leaving them no choice but to keep going.

The sun was well on its way down by the time they reached the top, only to find another obstacle: the lava flow had run over the edge of the cliff and, like the last one, had resulted in a sheer curtain. This one, at least, was only six or seven feet tall, but after their exhausting climb it may as well have been six hundred.

They stopped again, drinking sparingly from their water bottles, contemplating the surface of the curtain. The lava had cooled and cracked leaving a few hand holds but, after the climb, it was still going to be difficult.

"It'll be easier if you boost me up first," Connor said. "Pass me the backpacks then I'll help pull you up."

"What happens if there's nothing up there?" Blue-Wing asked.

"We'll camp there tonight if that's the case." She looked back down the steep slope, rubbing at her thighs to prevent them from cramping. "There's no way I'm going back down that and across those rocks twice in one day."

A rope ladder suddenly clattered down the lava flow and hung there.

"Do not exert yourselves unnecessarily, Marshals," a man's voice said from above them. "Please, climb up and we'll talk."

Connor and Blue-Wing looked at each other, both of them drawing their pistols.

She took hold of the rungs and lifted herself up, peeking over the top of the lava curtain, her pistol ready.

A Stranger stood a few feet away, watching her. He wore a full length cloak which covered his whole frame, making it impossible for her to see if he was armed.

"I mean you no harm, Marshall," he said. "If such was my intent, I could have shot you and your partner as you climbed up."

Connor weighed up her options, her aching legs beginning to tremble and cramp as she hung there, then lifted herself up and over the lip of the curtain.

"You must be Saxon."

The Stranger bowed a little, smiling at his own theatrics.

"I am indeed. Again, I stress I mean you no harm. Why don't you and your friend rest your weary legs and join me for something to eat?" His cloak parted as he lifted an arm to indicate a small camp, the fire made up but not lit. Tin plates with bread, cheese and pickles were placed around it along with three tin mugs. Next to the fire was a good-sized flagon of ale.

Connor turned slightly, never taking her eyes off Saxon.

"Daniel? Get up here."

As the other Marshall climbed up, Saxon moved over to the camp and sat. He took the flagon and poured the ale into the mugs, looking up at the Marshals as they took their places.

"Would you like the fire lit?" he asked them.

"Why not?" Connor said.

Instead of reaching for a tinder box, Saxon muttered a few words and waved his hand gently. The fire popped alight and in just a few moments, the wood was ablaze.

"You're a wizard?" Blue-Wing asked, his eyes wide. Saxon was obviously the first magic user he'd seen.

"Wizard's too grand a title for the small level of skill I have," Saxon replied. "A good fire's needed in the Wastes, though, if we're to talk."

"And why is that?" Connor asked.

Saxon sipped from his mug. "A fire, especially a camp fire out in the middle of nowhere, is something of an aide to the telling of tales. Most good tales take place around a fire of one sort or another in this Land in my experience."

"And what's your story? A claim of innocence about the hunters you've been luring out here?"

Connor took some bread and cheese and began to eat, Blue-Wing following her lead.

"I am indeed innocent of that, Marshall, as there have been no hunters. The people I have led here, to this plateau and the lake over yonder, have all come willingly."

Both Marshals looked over to where Saxon had pointed. What they had both taken to be the flat stone of the plateau, on closer inspection, was a large expanse of still, dark water. Barely a single ripple betrayed it for what it was and, despite the afternoon sky still being quite bright and clear, it held no reflection.

"So why do they come here?" Connor asked.

"To pray," Saxon said. "To pray and sacrifice themselves to their god."

The wind picked up, rising from a gentle, infrequent breeze, to a strong, almost gale force.

Still the lake's surface remained motionless.

The Marshals' coats and Saxon's cloak began to snap in the gusts. Blue-Wing's mug toppled over at his feet and spilled his ale. Connor had to grab at her hat to keep it on her head.

"Is this your doing?" she called to Saxon, raising her voice over the wind. Howls and shrieks came from the direction of the lake and she found herself wondering if it was just the wind blowing through the rocks.

"Not I, Marshall," Saxon said, standing up. He pulled his cloak tighter around himself. "It is the god of the lake. My god."

He left the camp fire which had been scattered in a burst of sparks and ash, and headed towards the calm waters.

"What do we do?" Blue-Wing called against the wind.

"I don't know," Connor called back, looking after the Stranger. "Come on."

They both stood and followed Saxon, walking across the plateau's surface to the edge of the lake where he waited.

"It is no coincidence that you come here, Marshall. The end is coming and you have long been destined to play a part in it."

"What are you talking about?"

The shrieking of the wind – if that was all it was – was joined by another sound: low and mournful, rhythmic and yet broken. Connor stared at the lake, fearful that she recognised the sound.

"My god, Great R'lyeh, has waited for you for so long," Saxon shouted. "He told me that you would come, that the Ruiner would lead you astray from one path only to have you fall unknowingly to this one."

The surface of the water broke, men and women rising from the depths. Water ran from their mouths as they opened them, drowned chants bubbling up from their throats. Their skin was white and wrinkled, their eyes rolled up in their sockets. A thin scum clung to the remains of their clothes and ran down their faces.

Connor and Blue-Wing stepped back, their coats flying out behind them, and drew their pistols.

"The sacrifices rise, Marshall. The followers of R'lyeh herald his coming."

As the dead reached the shoreline, ankle deep in water, they stopped, each of them looking blankly at Connor. The chanting, made with waterlogged throats, continued as the lake's surface behind them heaved and broke.

A huge, glistening dome rose up, white plumes of lake water cascading down its sides. Tentacles, each as thick as a man, rose up from beneath it, covered on all sides by suckers that twitched in the air, snapping their teeth. Flaps of ragged skin stretched between the tentacles almost forming wings of flesh between them. Another, smaller dome rose up in front of the main body, the head of the creature.

Connor gasped as not one but many eyes, multi-faceted and too numerous to count, were revealed, covering the top of the head. Beneath them, surrounded by a beard of writhing tentacles, was its mouth – dark and huge, lined with more teeth than seemed possible, it opened and closed, spitting water and drool to the lake below.

The thing squatted in the lake like a huge spider, its gaze fixed on Connor.

"Great R'lyeh! He comes for you!" Saxon shouted over the wind.

"Not . . . real," Blue-Wing gasped.

The god's eyes turned to him and Connor saw the top of its head pulse. She felt something in her mind, an image that came from outside but which seemed to have a physical force. It was glancing, leaving her with a headache and a sense of guilty gratitude that she had not felt the full effect.

Blue-Wing screamed and dropped to his knees, his hands grasping his head.

"Daniel!" Connor cried but stopped when Saxon raised his hand.

"The penalty of disbelief!" he shouted.

Blue-Wing looked at her through his gloved fingers and laughed, his eyes wide. He whipped his head around, looking over his shoulder.

"I see you!" he cried. "The Ruiner! The Ender!"

Connor looked behind them but saw only the expanse of the Funeral Wastes. She turned back to Blue-Wing in time to see him grab the pistol that had fallen to the floor, place it in his mouth and pull the trigger.

The back of his head burst with a spray of blood and bone before he toppled on to his side.

With instinct born of anger, Connor raised her pistol and fired at Saxon. She saw the bullet hit his chest, crumple and fall uselessly to the floor.

"My god protects me, Marshall," Saxon shouted. "Listen to him. Hear his words."

Connor turned back to the hulking thing in the lake, meeting its gaze.

Over the noise of the wind and the chorus of the drowned, R'lyeh's voice could be heard in her mind.

Saxon watched as the Marshall's mouth opened, a thin line of spit falling out the side. Her eyes rolled back in their sockets and she slumped to her knees, staying there for a moment before falling face first into the ground.

Connor woke to find her horse nuzzling her face. She pushed it away and carefully sat up, her head pounding. She touched her forehead and brought away dried blood.

"You took a fall, Marshall, but you should be fine."

Saxon sat on a rock opposite her, eating a sandwich. They were at the camp she and Blue-Wing had made before heading across the rocks to the path.

"It was real, then," she said, not bothering to make it a question. "How did I get down here? More sorcery?"

"No, Marshall, I carried you. Believe me, I'm glad you're as thin as you are."

Connor stood and looked around. A couple of miles away, across the broken and jagged boulders, was the lava flow that led up to the plateau and the lake. And Blue-Wing's body.

"My partner?"

"He is now part of the Choir of R'lyeh," Saxon said. "He will sing the praises of my god until the end of the Land."

"That might not be that long."

They looked at each other, the Marshall and the Stranger.

"My god did not tell me what he wanted you for, Marshall. Whatever he told you was for you only."

Connor rubbed gently at her head again, trying to brush away the blood she felt on her brow.

"I hate your god, Saxon. I could easily learn to hate you. But that. . . thing in the lake . . . the son of a bitch wants me to save the Land."

"Did he tell you how?" Saxon asked.

"Sure. All I need to do is kill another god."

They stared at each other again, Connor wishing she could laugh.

"It's probably best if we get going, then," Saxon said. He fed the remains of his sandwich to Blue-Wing's horse and then mounted it. "Where to, Marshall?"

Connor scratched at her head again, thinking of Blue-Wing, her father and Julia, even McKinley. A tear formed at the corner of one eye and rolled down her cheek.

"South," she said.

CABLE

"**S**tranger comin'."

I looked to my right, down the Main Street and, sure enough, a Stranger was making his way towards us. He staggered and stumbled, weaving from side to side. Other townsfolk watched him, a few of them making their way to him only to be pushed away. As he neared us, we could see the front of his shirt was drenched in blood; it had run from his chest, over his belt and down his trousers.

"Sweet Judas, will you look at the state of him," my Pa said. We both stood up on the Station's porch, amazed that anyone who had lost so much blood was still walking. Our wits returned quickly, though, and we rushed down the steps and into the street.

The Stranger managed to stumble over to us before dropping to his knees. He looked up as we reached him, kneeling beside him and half lifting, half dragging him to the Station. His face was drenched with sweat, his lips a stark purple against his pale skin.

"This . . . Cable?" he muttered.

"Yes son," Pa replied. "Curtis, go get Doc Valentine. Tell him to get his ass over here now."

I helped get the Stranger to the Station's porch then ran as fast as I could to the Doc's house.

By the time we got back, a couple of the townsfolk – it was the Waynes, Thomas being a fair doctor himself and his wife Martha had acted as a nurse before now – had helped Pa get the

128

Stranger inside and laid on one of the tables. His chest was surrounded by towels, all of which were soaked in blood, and my father just kept adding more.

"Judas Christ, Jonathan!" Doc Valentine said as he made his way through the small crowd of townsfolk who'd followed Stranger inside. "He can't still be alive?"

"He is, Harry, and I'll be damned if I know how. Never seen a man lose so much blood and keep on living."

Pa told me to move the blood soaked towels as he and Doc Valentine, with Thomas Wayne helping when needed, tended to the Stranger. Most of the people left when they realised there was nothing they could do to help; they weren't the sort to stay and watch or get in the way. A couple of them did help me deal with the towels and even started washing them. All the while, though, I kept an eye on the Stranger.

"Damn, Jonathan," Doc Valentine said about an hour or so later, wiping his brow and stepping back. "I have no idea how this man is still alive."

I stepped up behind my Pa and looked over his shoulder. There were bullet holes in the Stranger's chest that the Doc had sewn up; alone they might have been treatable. It was the huge amount of blood that was baffling them, however. As the three men had moved around the table to get a better angle to clean, stitch and dress the wounds, their feet had splashed in the blood on the floor.

"Never seen the like of it," Thomas said, drying his hands on one of the last clean cloths.

Despite his wounds and blood loss, the Stranger slept, his ruined chest rising and falling smoothly.

"The boy should be dead," Pa said.

He stirred at the words, opening his eyes, turning his head to look at us.

"Is this Cable?" he asked, his voice steady if not strong.

"It is, son," my Pa said, repeating the same answer he'd given earlier. "How are you feeling?"

The Stranger licked his lips. "Tired. Thirsty."

"We'll get you some water in a minute," Doc Valentine said. "Frankly, we're amazed you're still alive."

"What's your name, Stranger?" Pa asked, placing a comforting hand on his shoulder.

"Justice," the Stranger said. "My name's Justice."

We get a fair few Strangers through our town; it's one of the largest this far South in the Mainland Kingdoms so most people are used to them and pay them no mind. We've got a big Station that my Pa and I run and, on occasion, we've had to put some Strangers in rooms above the bar across the street when we run out of space.

This Stranger, though, caused a bit of a stir due to the manner of his arrival. Over the next few days, we had townsfolk popping by to see how he was doing. For the most part, this was genuine concern: folk in Cable are good natured and don't like to see anyone suffer if they can help it. Sure, there was a fair amount of curiosity in their visits, too, but you could hardly blame them. Strangers walking in from the plains covered in blood weren't that common round these parts.

Doc Valentine came to the Station twice a day for the first couple of days; impressed with the progress Justice was making, he dropped it to just one visit in the evening. I say "impressed" but amazed might be a better word. The Stranger's wounds were healed by the third day and, by the next evening, there were barely any scars. He was able to get up and walk around his room and was eating heartily by that time, leaving the Doc scratching his head.

"Never seen anything like it," he said to me and Pa on the fourth evening, after he'd removed Justice's stitches. "That young man should be laid in my surgery fighting for his life."

"I know what you mean, Harry," Pa said. "I've heard of one or two Strangers who could heal others with that magic of theirs. Never seen nor heard of one doing it to themselves."

"I wonder who did it to him. Shot him, I mean," I said.

"How many bullets did you pull out of him?"

The Doc shook his head. "Only two, but those were the only ones left in him. Two others had gone clean through and come out the back, along with more than a little bone and lung."

He sat back in his chair and gazed at the fireplace, shaking his head again.

"I just don't understand it," he said.

The morning after was the first time Justice came downstairs since he'd been moved up to one of the rooms after being stitched together. He walked slowly, there was no doubt of that, but he was walking.

I was behind the counter at the time, tallying up the number of Strangers we'd had pass through the Season before. At the time of Justice's arrival, we were in a quiet period; he was the only one in the Station at that point, the last one before him having left weeks before.

"How are you feeling?" I asked him as he took a seat at one of the tables near the fire place.

"Sore. Definitely sore." I offered and then made him a coffee, as well as one for myself, then sat with him. I rolled a jay and offered him one but he refused. "Not with my chest like this," he said with a rueful smile.

"Do you know who shot you?" I asked. "The Sheriff's kinda curious."

"Really?"

"Well, him and just about everyone else," I admitted. "Myself included."

Justice shook his head slowly. He had an expression on his face that seemed to be a mixture of confusion and regret.

"No, can't say as I do," he said after a moment's pause. "I remember facing off against someone, someone I'd been looking for, but after that . . . after that there was the sound of gunfire and then a voice, telling me I had to come here, to Cable. Told me other stuff, too. Next thing I know, I was walking towards this town, bleeding."

"Doc Valentine reckons you should be dead. You lost a lot of blood; I should know, he kept on and on about it," I said, puffing on my jay. It was my one vice, and then only occasionally, as I didn't drink much and wasn't attached to a lady at the moment, more's the pity. "You recognise that voice telling you to come here?"

"Nope, never heard it before," he said with a furtive look.

We were silent for a while, Justice staring into the ashes in the fire grate, myself smoking and listening to the sounds of the town outside. Though the day was warm for the start of the Season, there was an occasional breeze that carried voices or other noises to us. If the wind was in the right direction, the hammering of the blacksmith could be heard; the odd carriage drove past, the wheels crunching on the gravel spread over the earth of the roadway; laughter and swearing were both carried on the wind, as well as the badly played piano from the bar.

All in all, with the exception of Justice's almost miraculous recovery, it was a normal day in Cable.

I drained my coffee and put the remains of my jay out in the dregs at the bottom of the mug.

"I've got chores to be getting on with," I said, standing up. "You need anything, just yell. I'll be around here somewhere."

"Sure, thanks," he said, not really listening. He rubbed at his chest again. "Is there a church in town?" he asked, almost embarrassed.

"We've got two. There's the Judan chapel three streets over; go on up the Main Street, take a right at the bar and it's in front of you at the end of William Street. Keep going up Main Street to the town square, though, and take Bonny Road directly opposite you, then the third right into Custer Way and halfway along there, just before you get to the town's edge, there's a church of the Cuckoo God," I frowned at him. "Can't say I've heard of many Strangers having any sort of faith before."

He stood and rubbed at his chest again. Slowly, he went back upstairs to his room; I shrugged and carried on with what I'd been doing. Five minutes later, he came back down; Pa and I had found him some old clothes to replace his ruined ones and he wore these when he left. I stepped over to the front window and watched him head up the street and take a right at the bar.

While he was gone, my Pa returned from the shopping trip he'd been on. He'd bought food and such figuring – rightly as it turned out – that when one Stranger appeared, others did. He asked after Justice and seem surprised when I said he'd apparently gone to chapel.

"Ain't that many Strangers I've known take to religion," he said as we unpacked the tins of beans, bags of flour and other bits and pieces.

"Said the same thing to him. We've had a few over the years, but not many," I said. "There was that one, Crypt, who seemed more of a preacher than Father Cassidy."

Pa laughed as he remembered him. "Hell, yeah. Spent the whole time he was here trying to convert the other Strangers. Least he did till that one, Fade, popped him in the mouth. Never seen a woman hit so hard."

The bell on the reception desk rang and I left Pa to unpack the rest as I went out to the front.

Three Strangers stood waiting, their long coats and hats dusty from the road. Each of them had packs slung on their backs and I could see gun belts around their waists. Time was most Strangers didn't carry guns but, over the years and Seasons, things had changed. Throughout the Mainland Kingdoms, tolerance towards them had waned; as more and more of them were set upon or even killed by Natives, more and more of them had taken to wearing arms.

One of the three was a woman, a fair bit younger than my own forty years, and the first female Stranger I'd seen in a long time. The other two were men, both of them bearded, and all three were tanned by the sun.

"Howdy," I said. "Welcome to Cable. You three planning on staying a while?"

"A couple of days," one of the men said. "Stock up on supplies, rest a while, then head on again. Do you have rooms for all three of us?"

"Sure do, Stranger. If you'd like to sign in, I can show you straight up."

I turned the register, a big leather bound book, around to him and handed him the pen.

"Do you have a stable for our horses?" he asked, writing the three names on the page.

"Not a problem," I glanced out of the front window at the three horses tied to the hitching post. "It's just out the back. Once I've shown you to your rooms, I'll take them round."

He handed the pen back and I turned the register back to me.

"Must be a quiet time for you," he said. "We the first Strangers you've had this Season?"

I looked at the page and smiled. "No, we've got one other in at the moment but, with all the excitement of his arrival, I guess I forgot to get him signed in."

I wrote in Justice's name and room number below those of the new arrivals then looked up at them. The one who'd done the talking looked from the register to me and then to his friends.

"Seems there's a Stranger called Justice staying here," he said to them. The other two swapped glances.

"Not the most common of names but it's probably someone else," the other man said.

"Probably? I'd say it's got to be," the woman replied.

The first Stranger turned back to me.

"Is Justice around?"

"No, he's out," I looked at each of them in turn. "There isn't going to be any trouble, is there?"

"No, no trouble. When he gets back in, tell him Slake says howdy. If he doesn't know my name then it's not who we think it is. If he does . . ."

"Then we need to have a chat with him," the other man said.

"Let me show you to your rooms and then I'll sort out your

horses. If I see Justice when he returns, I'll pass on your message."

"Much obliged," Slake said.

As it turned out, there was no need for me to say anything. Later that afternoon, Slake and his friends – the man was called Dale, the woman Cross – were sat in the common room, the area in front of reception. I think it likely they'd done so deliberately to get a look at Justice who helped them out by returning from church.

"Curtis," he said to me as he walked past the reception counter. He glanced over at the other Strangers and nodded at them but said nothing. Dale, however, did.

"Holy crap," his face was a picture: his eyes were wide and his mouth open, his skin pale.

"I don't believe it," Cross said, staring at Justice.

He paused at the desk, looking back at them.

"Hey kid," Slake said, the only one of the three to have kept his composure. "Thought you were dead."

I leaned round the desk to get a better look at Justice. After the way he'd arrived at the Station and the days I'd spent helping him heal, I'd got to like the guy.

He looked confused at first, his gaze moving from one to the other, frowning in concentration. All of a sudden, his face cleared and he gasped, staggering slightly.

"You okay, Justice?" I asked, putting a hand out to stabilise him.

"Hook," he said quietly, then slumped to the floor.

Dale and Cross rushed over and the three of us managed to lift his slim frame over to the nearest chair.

"Get him some water," Slake told me and without thinking about it, I went into the kitchen to get him a drink. When I returned, they were all sat around the same table, Justice resting his head on his arms. He lifted his head and sipped at the water a little.

"Who's Hook?" I asked Slake.

"Hook's the Stranger who shot and killed him just over three Seasons ago," he said.

"Killed him?"

"Yep," Dale said, taking some papers and tobacco from his waistcoat. "We were all there, outside an abandoned convent way up North," he rolled a jay and lit it. "The kid here wanted to face off against another Stranger, named Hook. Trouble was, he had some friends: the Ivory Gang. Heard of them?"

I nodded. Just about every Station Master I'd met knew of them.

"Justice's little talk with Hook didn't go so well," Cross said, not unkindly. "Ended up with him being shot four or five times in the chest."

"Long story short," Slake said. "Justice was killed. Double checked him myself."

The four of us sat and looked at Justice who, perhaps because of the silence, raised his head and sat back in his chair. He ran both hands over his face, colour coming back into his cheeks, before looking around the table.

"I remember now," he said. "Speaking with Hook, hoping to learn about my parents, him shooting me. Then the voice."

"Voice?" Slake asked.

"The voice of Judas. He spoke to me, brought me back from the dead. Told me to come here."

"Judas?" Dale said. "As in Judas Christ, the Stranger who was hanged 1800 years ago? Supposedly became a god after his death? That Judas?"

Justice ignored his sarcasm. "You ever hear of anything like this?" he asked Slake.

The Stranger picked up Dale's paper and rolled himself a jay.

"People coming back from the dead isn't an every day event. I've heard of three or four times it's happened; even seen one guy years after he was supposed to have been killed, but this is the first time I know for definite that it's happened. As to the whole voice of Judas, thing . . . damned if I know," he stared at Justice.

"You were a Native once, kid. What was your name?"

"Jimmy Hayfield," Justice said with a small smile. "Checking I am who I say I am?"

"Pretty much," Slake said. "Stranger things have happened."

We all sat and watched Justice as he drank the water I'd given him. As Slake had said, resurrection wasn't a daily occurrence but I'd heard stories of it happening as well. There were tales of both Strangers and Natives who'd come back from the dead in one way or another; the Natives from the Blue States in the South held that the dead could be raised deliberately. It was said that anything killed in the Funeral Wastes would return to life. And, of course, there was the tale of Judas Christ's betrayer who, consumed with guilt over her betrayal of Christ, had given herself up to the law. She had been executed but, as punishment, was condemned to return to life again and again in eternal sufferance. The story claimed she'd been killed countless times, only to return to life, damned for all eternity.

"So what now?" Justice asked.

Both Cross and Dale looked at Slake, making it clear that he was the man in charge.

He shrugged, puffing on his jay to keep its embers glowing.

"We're headed South in a day or two. Plan on getting to the Blue States by next Season. You're welcome to join us again," he chuckled, a dry sound without much humour. "As long as we don't run into your old friends."

"Don't say that," Dale said. "That's just asking for trouble."

"He's right," Cross said. "You say something like that and the next thing you know, Hook's walking through the door."

"You called?"

We all turned to the kitchen door where Pa stood, arms crossed, a big smile on his face.

"I'm sorry," he said, laughing and holding up a hand. "Heard the end of your talk and couldn't resist taking advantage."

"Sweet Judas, Pa, you scared the crap out of us. Haven't you got anything better to do?"

The Strangers gathered at the table laughed and, for perhaps the last time that Season, I thought things were okay.

The next day passed quietly, just another day in Cable. People went to work, kids went to school, the faithful went to church, men and women went about their day. Things were good in Cable that day, though I didn't get to sample too much of it: the plumbing – what there was of it – broke in the Station and, while the rest of the town enjoyed the Seasonable weather, I was getting soaked repairing pipes under the kitchen sink. With all that happened since then, I think I'd rather spend the rest of my life swimming in dish water than go through it all again.

The next morning, six days after Justice had stumbled in from the plains, we had another Stranger ride into town. Unlike every other Stranger we'd ever seen, however, this one ignored the Station and rode his horse straight to the Sheriff's office. I was sat out on the porch with my Pa and we watched him ride up Main Street, the hood of his cloak pulled up and hiding his face. The cloak covered most of his legs and strapped to the saddle behind him was a bed roll and pack.

The Stranger was followed a minute or two later by another rider; with the hat and coat she wore, it took us a moment to realise the rider was a woman. Though the Stranger had arrived first, he waited for her to join him before dismounting and tying up both horses. Once that was done, they both walked into Sheriff Freewood's office.

"Ain't that a peculiar sight?" Pa said. "I'd be willing to bet that woman wasn't a Stranger but she's sure riding with one."

"Damndest thing," I agreed. Running the Station as long as we had, we were pretty good at spotting a Stranger. There's always something about them; not just the manner of their dress, as some of them look like Natives; not just their names, as odd and overly dramatic as some of them can be. A Stranger stands out somehow, some mix of arrogance and disinterest that sets them apart from Natives and Walkers.

138

The pair didn't come out of Sheriff Freewood's office for some time; I had things to do around the Station, but my Pa was sat out there most of the morning. The two horses remained outside at the hitching post, the riders inside.

"Five Strangers in a week," Slake said as I walked into the Station. He was stood at the window and had obviously seen the new arrivals. "Getting kinda busy round here."

"We've had busier times," I said, keeping my tone light. Slake was something of a grim man and almost everything he said was stated in dire tones.

"I've a feeling you might get busier."

"What makes you say that?" I asked.

He pointed across and up the street at the Sheriff's office.

"Stranger who just turned up, his name's Saxon. Dale knows him from way back and I've had a few run-ins with him as well. Serious fella, never does anything for fun, there's always a reason. Big on religion, too, worships that water god, R'lyeh. If he's in town, something's up."

"Can't say I follow you, Slake," I said and I was being honest.

"Saxon never comes into towns, or at least very rarely. Twice I've heard of him staying somewhere, and both times it's ended in bloodshed with him in the middle." He stepped away from the window and headed for the stairs. "We'll be on our way tomorrow, I think," he said and walked up to his room.

I shook my head and smiled at the ominous nature of Slake's words. He wasn't the first Stranger I'd known with a propensity for melodrama. Used to being viewed as strange beings, rumoured to be devils, wizards or gods, some of them became a little too caught up in themselves. We once had one Stranger pass through preaching that the end of the Land was due in a few days. All these Seasons later, the Land was still here.

Later that evening, Saxon came into the Station. Pa was at the counter when he did; I was in the kitchen cooking up the evening meal for our other guests.

"Howdy," he said, putting his pack on the floor. "I need a

room for a night."

I looked through the doorway as Saxon pushed his hood back with both hands. His face was lean and weather-worn like many Strangers, and he wore a beard which he obviously kept trimmed as best he could. His hair was shaggy, curling at the ends, and a dark brown in colour.

"Not a problem," Pa said, turning the register round to him. "Saw you and your friend arrive earlier. Will she be joining you?"

"No, she's a King's Marshall," Saxon said, writing his name in the register. "Something of a full house here," he said, pointing at the names of the other Strangers.

"There have been times when it's been busier, but we're doing okay at the moment," Pa said. He handed Saxon the key to his room. "I'll take you up to your room if you like."

"That's okay, I'll find it."

He shouldered his pack and walked to the stairs; only a few minutes later, he came back.

"Is there a problem with the room, Stranger?" Pas asked him. He still makes all the beds himself despite the lifting and pulling it entails and he gets very sensitive about any criticism.

"The room's fine," Saxon said. "Would you tell the others I'll be in the bar across the street and I'd like them to join me?"

"The others? You mean the other Strangers?"

"Yes indeed. I'll be there all night and would like to speak with them," with that, he left the Station.

"When did I become a damn secretary?" Pa grumbled.

"Told you we should have hired Doc Valentine's daughter," I called through to him.

He came into the kitchen, a worried expression on his face.

"You heard what that Saxon fella said?" he asked. "I don't like this, Curtis, not at all. Justice turning up all shot to hell, bleeding everywhere while the Doc worked on him and then miraculously recovering. Them three Strangers turning up on top of that, saying they'd seen the boy shot dead. Now this Saxon fella riding in with a King's Marshall in tow. You ever hear of a

Stranger riding with a Marshall?"

"No, Pa."

"Me neither. It ain't right, son. It feels like . . ."

"Like something's brewing up, waiting to happen?" I finished.

"Yeah. That or like pieces being pushed together like a puzzle." He stood, leaning against one of the cupboards, watching as I gently stirred the spiced chicken I'd cooked. "Go on up to their rooms, son, and pass on Saxon's message," he said finally. "I'll take care of the chicken. If they go to the bar, head over with them. I want to know what the hell's going on."

"You sure?"

"They're staying in my damn Station, I got a right to know what they're planning."

I realised that my Pa actually sounded a little scared about then. He'd owned the Station since before I was born and had dealt with more Strangers than I ever would; as the Seasons went by, their numbers were declining. I'd seen him scared of them before now – he was a smart man and knew when he had a bad one in the place – but I think this was the first time I'd seen him really unnerved. I think he knew something was coming but also knew that there was nothing he could do about it.

"No problem, Pa," I took off the stained apron I wore when cooking and tossed it over to him. "Just don't ruin my chicken, you hear?" I said, trying to lighten the mood.

"Go on, get the hell out of here," he said, tying the apron around his waist. "Find out what you can from them damn Strangers, especially that Saxon." He picked up the wooden spoon from the pot and tasted the sauce. "And find out if one of them knows how to make a decent spiced chicken," he called after me as I left the kitchen.

The top of the stairs opened out on to a roughly square landing, two rooms each on the left and right with a corridor ahead. That corridor became a T junction with more rooms off both branches. As Justice and the others were the first Strangers of the Season, they'd been given the first rooms on the landing.

141

I knocked on room number two first; it was Slake's room and, as he appeared to be in charge of the others, I figured he was the best place to start.

He opened the door and stared at me, a little bleary eyed as if he hadn't long woken. I passed on Saxon's message and he sighed as I finished.

"Fine," he said. "We all chase after Saxon again."

"Again?"

"Long story, happened in the bad old days," he scratched at his beard. "Go knock the others up, tell them I'll meet them downstairs," He closed the door, leaving me on the landing.

I did as he asked, getting a tired look from Justice as if he'd seen this all before. There was no answer from Cross's door and I originally thought she might be asleep. However, when Dale answered the door to his room shirtless and sweaty, wearing only his under things, I put two and two together. He swore in a very creative manner when I passed on the message and slammed the door in my face. Five minutes later, though, we were all stood at reception. Each of the Strangers, except Justice, were wearing their guns.

"You coming with us?" Slake asked as we all headed out the door.

"Sure am," I said. "Pa and I want to make sure nothing. . . untoward is being planned. You stay in this Station, you're our responsibility."

"Been a while since I had a babysitter," Dale said, his mood having improved since I interrupted him. "Might be fun. Come on, let's go find out what big, old mysterious Saxon wants."

"Things might get a little hairy in there," Slake said, looking not at me but at Justice and Cross. "You want to sit this out, we wouldn't think less of you."

"You ain't ditching me that easy," Cross said with a smile at Dale. Slake turned to Justice.

"Kid?"

"After everything I've been through, one more fight in a bar isn't going to make much difference."

Slake nodded and stepped down from the Station's porch onto the gravelled road, his boots crunching on the surface. The bar was across from the Station and a few houses up, on the corner of the street. Much like every other bar I'd seen in the few other towns I'd been to, it had swing doors, a bar against the opposite wall and round tables with chairs between the two. Nothing fancy about it, the place existed to sell drinks to the Natives after a long day of work and to the few Strangers who wandered it. Its existence based purely on its function, it was called The Tap but no-one bothered with that – it was just 'the bar.' The only thing that set it apart was the awful piano player, Big Ritchie who was just competent enough to be forgiven, but bad enough to be annoying.

A few of the patrons, and there were a lot tonight, turned to give us a cursory look as we walked in, but there was no animosity. We scanned the tables, looking for Saxon and, after Dale spotted him, all except Slake and Dale went over to his table while the other pair bought drinks.

Saxon was sat with a woman who looked lean but confident and not just because of the eight pointed star she wore on her chest. Her short hair was spiky as if she hadn't long removed her hat and, as she kicked a chair across to us, we all saw the gun she wore.

"Take a seat, folks," she said, looking from one to the other.

Justice sat down as Cross and I asked other people if chairs were spare, dragging them from other tables. Most people were happy enough to give up seats, though there were a fair number of curious looks; Strangers and a King's Marshall getting together was an unusual event. By the time Dale and Slake returned with a couple of pitchers of beer and some glasses, though, we had enough seats for everyone.

"Well this is cosy," Dale said, pouring out some beers.

"And why is the Station Master here?" Saxon asked Slake, ignoring me completely.

"I'm here to find out what your plans are and how they affect me, my Pa and the Station," I said before Slake could reply. "Any other questions about me, feel free to ask me direct."

"Still haven't lost that way with people, eh Saxon?" Dale chuckled.

"You seem cheery for a Stranger sat with a King's Marshall who happens to know there's an arrest warrant out for you," the Marshall said. "You too, Slake," she turned to Cross. "I don't know your name but I'm willing to bet you're the third Stranger connected to Sheriff Tidyman's death in Anchorhead."

Cross looked at her hands, turning her beer glass around, ignoring the Marshall.

"I killed Tidyman," Slake said. "These pair weren't even in the building when I did it."

The Marshall looked at Justice. "You I don't know, except from the stories Sheriff Freewood's told me: the Stranger who showed up, shot to hell, but managed to survive. What's your story, Justice? Why are you running with Slake's gang?"

"And when did it become your gang?" Dale interrupted.

"Cross and I took a vote. You lost," he said. "So now the veiled threats and intros are out of the way, how's about our good friend Saxon here tells us what's so damned important?"

Each of us turned to face the Stranger who had pushed his hood back so it formed a small pillow at his neck. He leaned forward, his elbows on the table, his hands clasped together.

"The End has begun," he said simply. "I have received word that the Land is going to cease. The Ruiner, the End Timer approaches and all will fall before him."

We were silent for a moment, expecting more but Saxon remained quiet.

"Well, that's put a downer on the evening," Dale said. He poured himself another drink and offered up the pitcher. "Anyone? One more drink before the Land ends?"

"Who have you had this message from?" Slake asked.

"Great R'lyeh himself. He seeks to prevent the demise of

144

everything which will, of course, include himself."

"So a god is speaking to you?" Cross asked him. She shook her head and sat back in her seat. "Like I haven't seen enough religious lunatics," she said to Dale and Slake.

"Where do you sit with this, Marshall?"

For the first time since we'd met her, I saw the Marshall fidget, and her gaze dropped to the table.

"Saxon's right," she said. "I've seen . . . I've seen R'lyeh. Heard him." She looked up and scanned our faces one after another. "Something is coming. Something terrible. An ancient god, empowered by the spirits of those he has deceived through the ages. He is coming to put an end to us all."

Dale pointed at Justice who sat opposite him.

"Looks like you picked the wrong time to come back from the dead, kid."

"Shut up, Dale," Slake said. "This god have a name?" he asked the Marshall.

Before she could reply, there was a crash of glass behind us followed by shouts and cheers. We all looked over to where a man, short and stout, had climbed on to a table. He wore a simple, black cassock, tied at the waist with a red rope. His hair was long and curly but tied back in a simple pony-tail and he wore a full beard. Both arms were outstretched and in one hand he clutched a book.

"Brothers and sisters!" he shouted above the noise. The people who were sat at his table stood and tried to get him down but he resisted them. "Brothers and sisters, hear me!" he shouted, standing firm on the table. "I bring you news to brighten your lives! News that will bring a smile to every face and lift the spirits of those in need!"

There were still people shouting and cat-calling the man, but their numbers dwindled as the good folk of Cable relented and let him have his say. Even those whose table he was stood upon had stopped in their attempts to move him.

"There is a change coming, my people, one that will free you from decision, from strife, from discord. It costs no money, it costs

145

neither sweat nor blood. This change will give you the opportunity to free yourself from your daily worries and concerns."

Dale nudged Slake to get his attention.

"Isn't that . . . ?"

"Yeah, it's him," they both turned to Cross who nodded and then to Justice who did the same.

"So what is this change?" a woman at the bar shouted. The man on the table spun round to face her.

"It is a glorious thing, a wondrous, marvellous thing. It is simply abandoning your old gods in favour of the one, true god."

The groans and shouts that greeted his words drowned him out for a moment, people turning back to their drinks. I leaned toward Justice.

"Who is he?"

"The Reverend Diver, devout Judan preacher. He's no love for Strangers, though."

"But Judas was a Stranger."

"Not according to Diver. Far as he's concerned, Christ was a Native through and through."

"Listen to me! Listen!" Diver shouted. "Each of us knows the Cuckoo God pays no attention to the Land or its creatures. Why then do people pray to it? No-one here has seen the Great R'lyeh who supposedly lays sleeping beneath a far off ocean that no-one has ever sailed upon. Why then do people pray to it?"

Dale turned to Saxon and the Marshall.

"You going to tell him or shall I?" he said with a wink.

"Judas Christ was hanged from a tree eighteen hundred years ago, a Stranger, a man killed by a long-forgotten empire. Why then do people pray to him?"

"I thought you said he was a Judan preacher?" I asked Justice.

"He was." He sat forward in his seat and I noticed the other Strangers were all watching Diver.

"All these gods and others, they don't exist. All these people with their wasted prayers. Who here would rather pray for something with the knowledge that they will receive it? Who here has a fervent prayer that they whisper into the night, knowing that their god is dead or doesn't care?"

"I pray Big Ritchie would learn to play that piano he murders every night!" a man at the bar shouted. Ritchie's reply, probably colourful, was lost in the laughter.

"Yeah, and I pray my Herb had a bigger tool between his legs!" The crowd roared at Mabel Corby's suggestion. She was somewhat notorious in town, carrying on with several men, having married her much older husband Herb for his money – or so the rumours went.

Others in the bar shouted out their prayers: more money; more women; more whisky. Each of them was greeted with laughter, Diver joining in with the crowd.

"Then meet me tomorrow at noon," he said as the suggestions petered out. "Speak with one another in the morning and meet me in the town square at noon. I will tell you of my god then."

The people watched him step down from the table, a little bemused at the sudden ending of his sermon. He left the bar and it quickly returned to normal, people laughing over their drinks at the old man. Big Ritchie struck up a tune which led to one man shouting out he hoped that prayer would come true sooner rather than later.

"Didn't the good Reverend Diver use to be a Judan?" Dale asked.

"Curtis was asking the same thing," Justice said. "Looks like he's had something of a change of heart."

"Seems odd he's preaching about a god without a name," Cross said. "Especially as Slake was just asking about the one you pair are so scared of." She looked at the Marshall and Saxon.

"They are one and the same. Diver's god is the Ender, the Ruiner, Locus and Loci, all points and the end point," Saxon said.

Slake took out his pouch and made himself a jay.

"Figured as much," he said.

There didn't seem much more to say after that. Dale became insistent that whatever fight Saxon had with Diver and his god was nothing to do with them; the Marshall threatened them with arrest if they tried to leave; Justice doubted that all them being there – himself most of all – was a coincidence.

Slake, though, had the last word.

"I've heard of this Loci before; he's something different from all of us, though I don't know if he's really a god. We'll stay a couple more days," He put his hand up to quiet Dale's protests. "This thing's going to play out anyway. We may as well see what we can do."

Saxon thanked him, passing on the blessings of great R'lyeh which Slake said he had no use for.

He left the bar with his gang, which now included Justice, leaving me with Saxon and the Marshall. Neither of them were much company as Saxon seemed intent on converting me while the Marshall sat quietly, nursing her drink. After a while, I made my excuses and left.

Outside, the sound of laughter and bad singing accompanying Big Ritchie's poor piano playing almost drowned out the sound of someone softly calling my name. I stopped at the corner of the bar and looked down the dark lane that separated it from Hardman's General Store.

Half-hidden in the shadows was a man, tall and skinny from what little I could see. The few lights that were on in the houses across the street, coupled with the candlelight coming through the bar's window didn't illuminate a whole lot.

"Did you call me, mister?" I asked.

"Sure did, Curtis," he said. He struck a match and lit the jay he had in his mouth. The bright yellow flame showed a thin face wearing a big smile before he blew it out.

"Can't say I know you, Stranger."

"Oh, I haven't been a Stranger for many, many Seasons, Curtis." He pushed himself away from the store's wall and walked over to me. He wore jeans, a shirt and jacket, much like every other man around these parts. What set his clothes apart, though, was that they were all made out of green and red patches, neatly shaped like diamonds. The colours alternated and while the outfit looked passable in the half-light of candles, I guessed it would be garish in the day time. To literally top it off, he wore a hat that had three large cones coming off it, one each to the left and right, and one out the top. At the end of each of these hung a small silver bell that tinkled softly as he walked.

"Hell of an outfit you got there, mister," I said. I held my ground even as he got closer than was strictly necessary, his smile never wavering. The nearer he came, the clearer I could see his eyes – they were bright and seemed to sparkle, reminding me of my uncle Victor in the last days of his life. He'd gone mad, shouting at people who weren't there, calling out for children he'd never fathered to help him. Difference was, this fella's eyes held more intelligence than uncle Victor had possessed even before he lost his mind.

"These old things?" he said, indicating his clothes. "My dear Curtis, you should have seen me when I started out. Oh, the colours were there, but there was no order to them. As you can see, however, all the unruly, untidy mess has been replaced," as he finished, he actually twirled in front of me.

"What do you want, mister?" I asked. "And how do you know my name?"

"A lucky guess: you just looked like a Curtis." He clasped his hands behind his back, turned on his heel and began walking up and down in front of me.

"What do I want? That's easy, my friend, absolutely easy. Those crazy Strangers you have tucked away in that Station of yours? I'd like them gone, out of town, cleared out. And I want them to take that skinny but lovely Marshall with them, too.

"Now I'm going to go right ahead and pre-empt your next question – which, with the startling lack of ingenuity and originality endemic to you people – is just bound to be 'Why?' and skip to the end and not tell you."

He stopped walking and talking in front of me and thrust his face close to mine.

"Yours is not to reason why, Curtis my lad. Yours is but to do or die."

"You threatening me?"

"Of course I am!" he said with a laugh. "The dramatic walking, the crazy talk, the word 'die' used as a warning? What part of that did you not understand?" He reached into his jacket and I instinctively went for my gun which I then remembered I hadn't worn.

Instead of a weapon, however, he pulled out a stick which had a miniature, cloth version of his own head and hat on the end. Even the bells were there, jingling softly.

"You go back to your Station, Curtis my boy, and you tell them Strangers to be on the road by ten of the clock tomorrow morning, okay? I see any of them around town after that and you get a visit from my little friend here." He waved the doll's head in front of me.

"And that's mean to scare me?"

"Damn straight it is!" the doll's head screamed in a thin, high voice. The cloth had changed to flesh, pulled tight over the tiny skull. The stump of the neck bled freely, blood pouring down the stick and dripping over the jester's fingers.

I cried out and stepped back, stumbling over my feet and falling on my ass.

"Looks like Curtis has gone for a trip," the jester said. The doll's head had become cloth once more, and the blood had vanished. He bent at the waist, his hands on his knees and smiled at me.

"You tell them Strangers to be moving on, you hear me Curtis? Get them gone."

He stood up and walked back into the alley, disappearing into the darkness, leaving me sat on my backside in the road.

The encounter with the lunatic jester shook me; I'd rather have dealt with half a dozen Strangers armed to the teeth and with each one pissed at me. It took a good few minutes to get myself together, helped by having a couple of drunkards stumble out of the bar and laugh at me.

I got up and dusted myself off and with a final glance down the alleyway – which appeared to be empty – I headed back to the Station. I thought Slake and the others might still be awake but when I asked my Pa, he said they'd all gone straight to their rooms, not even bothering to eat the chicken we'd prepared.

"You okay son? You look like hell."

"I've had better evenings, Pa, no doubt about that."

I told him about Saxon and his story, of the Marshall and Slake, and of the jester outside the bar.

"I don't think I've ever had such a shock," I said, thinking of the doll's head that had screamed at me.

My Pa sat at the table and sipped at the whisky he'd poured as I'd talked.

"Can't say I'm pleased about all this," he said. "I've heard stories of this Loci myself; a Stranger told me of him years ago, how he was supposed to be collecting followers in the mountains East of the Frontiers. Never put much stock in it till now."

"If he's East of the Frontiers at least we don't have much to worry about."

My Pa looked at me with an expression of love and pity.

"Son, Loci's already here. He's that jester you ran into."

I sighed and sipped at my own whisky.

"Damn it," I said.

The next morning, Pa and I were awake before the first of the Strangers came down for breakfast, despite the amount of whisky we'd ended up drinking the night before. Neither of us are hardened drinkers and it showed on both our faces. As I stumbled around the kitchen, I kept thinking to myself "You're still drunk. It's the next morning and you're still drunk."

One by one the Strangers made their way down for breakfast. It can be difficult running a Station; none of the Strangers pay anything and how much we get from the town's council is dependent on how many Strangers we had the Season before. With their numbers dwindling, we had less and less money each

Season to feed them or ourselves.

I took a plate of bacon, eggs, some beans in sauce and some fried potatoes over to Justice who was the last to arrive. Saxon hadn't made his way back to the Station the night before so it was just the four of them.

"Sorry to interrupt your breakfast," I said, handing Justice his plate and then pulling a chair over. "But I need to tell you something."

As they ate, I recounted what had happened after I left the bar. Once I'd finished, I mentioned what my Pa had said, about the jester being Loci. Slake nodded as I spoke.

"That certainly sounds like the description I've heard," he said. "The red and green clothes, the crazy talk." He shrugged and looked at the others. "Maybe there's something to what Saxon was saying last night."

"And you still want to wait around and find out?" Dale asked. "Sweet Judas, Slake! This Loci fella is a madman at best and a god at worst. Why the hell do we need to get involved? I say we get out of here."

"That's your choice, Dale. This Loci is weird, that's for certain, but if he wanted us gone, why appear to Curtis? Why not see us face to face?"

"He's scared, that's why," Cross said. She pushed her now empty plate away from her and patted her stomach. "Thanks, Curtis, that was great."

"I think he's scared, too," Slake said. "Or if not scared at the very least he's being careful. That means one of us – at least one of us – can hurt him."

Dale sat, shaking his head.

"You both sound as crazy as this Loci. What about you, kid?" he asked Justice.

"I say we wait and see what happens," he said around a mouthful of potatoes and beans. "See where all this goes."

Dale rolled a jay and headed over to the front door.

"This is all going to end in tears," he said and stepped out on to the porch.

* * *

A few hours later, we were all sat in the reception area, including Pa. The pair of us were feeling a lot better after having some food and were milling around, more interested in what might happen than completing our chores. The Strangers sat around, Slake, Dale and Cross playing cards, Justice reading a book he'd found somewhere. Saxon still hadn't called in despite his meagre belongings being locked in his room. Ten o'clock came and went and, despite the jester's warning, nothing happened.

Doc Valentine called in sometime after eleven, nodded at the Strangers and asked how Justice was feeling, before speaking to Pa at the reception desk. They whispered for a moment before Pa called to the rest of us.

"You may want to hear what the Doc has to say," he said.

"I was in the bar last night when that preacher started harking on about his one, true god. We don't get many of his sort through here, though we've had a few over the years. Anyway, I was there when he was talking about prayers and people started laughing and calling out their own.

"Mabel Corby shouted out for her husband Herb to be better equipped between the legs. She came to see me not an hour ago and had me go back to her house and examine Herb. The long and short of it – and I probably could have used a better phrase – is that her prayers appear to have been answered. I've been treating Herb since I became a doctor and I'm willing to swear that what he has between his legs this morning was no-where near as big yesterday."

We all swapped glances, hoping that no-one would laugh.

"The problem is, on the way to my house, Mabel told several friends. I'm guessing by now, they've each told several more and so on and so on. Other people at the bar have also claimed to have had their prayers answered: I saw young Edwin Roberts looking as happy as a pig in shit on my way over here. He married Lizzie Taskman not three weeks ago and told me they

153

woke up this morning to find her chest was enormous. That was the word he used: enormous. For a woman who, as of yesterday, was flatter than me, that's pretty good going."

"You got her address, Doc?" Dale asked with a big grin. Cross elbowed him in the side.

"Oh it's funny alright," Valentine said. "But if that preacher or his god are granting wishes, what are they going to cost? No-one gives anything for free, I don't care what that preacher said. And the more people who hear about these prayers coming true, the more of them are going to go see him in the town square."

"The Doc's right: you don't get something for nothing," Pa said. "These townsfolk who've had their wishes granted, they're going to want more. Those who didn't make any prayers are sure as hell going to be saying them now."

"That's how he gets them," Slake said. "In the story I heard, Loci's herald heals the sick; making prayers come true is much the same. Diver will almost certainly try and take your townsfolk away, off to join his god."

"I'll be damned if I'm going to let him do that," Doc Valentine said. "The people here are good folk; some of them might be easily tempted by getting something for free, but they're still good at heart." He looked at Slake. "Will you help us?"

"It's no coincidence, all this," Justice said. "Judas bringing me back from the dead, telling me to come here; the rest of you turning up; Diver coming to this town. It's got to be connected. I say we help."

"Can't say I like the idea of being part of someone else's plan," Dale said, scratching at the stubble on his chin. "And I have to admit that I'm more than willing to get out of this place. Reason or not, us all being here at the same time means nothing to me. I vote we leave."

Cross ran both hands through her hair, gently tugging at a knot she found.

"Justice's right. This whole things feels like it's connected with something. I vote for staying."

Myself, Pa and Doc Valentine all turned to Slake. He slowly rolled a jay and lit it, puffing away to get it going.

"That line I said in the bar last night, about us having a vote on calling this Slake's gang? It was a joke," he told the other Strangers. "We don't vote. We were quick enough to help Cross when she needed it. These people have asked for help. Least we can do is go along to the town square, see what happens with Reverend Diver."

"Think you're making a mistake, my friend," Dale said. "Saxon and that Marshall, hell even the kid here, they've messed up your head. All this talk of gods and prayers and magic . . . like I said earlier, this is all going to end bad. We're all going to regret staying here."

There was silence for a few minutes till Slake stood up.

"All of you who're coming, get what you need and lets make a move."

One by one, we all left reception. Pa and I went to our rooms and picked up our jackets.

"You okay with this Curtis?"

"Pa, I'm not sure what this is," I said. "Tell you the truth, that whole thing with Loci last night has kinda unsettled me. Since when do gods come to Cable?"

Pa put his arm round my shoulder and gave me a rough hug.

"We'll be alright, son."

We put our jackets on and, as I moved to the door, Pa stopped me.

"It might be best to have these," he said, opening a cupboard and taking out our guns. "Who knows what's going to happen?"

It came as no surprise to any of us to find the town square was full. Cable's a fair sized town with maybe a thousand or so Natives in it; it seemed like most of them had congregated in the square to hear Reverend Diver speak.

There was a small, round fountain in the centre. It was a simple thing, maybe ten feet across, with a column in the middle, decorated with various figures from the old stories. Out of the mouths of these figures poured water, falling into the basin where it was pumped round and back up the column.

The whole thing had been boarded over, however, and a platform constructed over it. A rough set of stairs led up to the top of the makeshift stage where Diver stood with another man, a Stranger. He was dressed entirely in black and hooded like Saxon but wore no cloak – his hood was part of his jacket and was large enough that his entire face was in shadow.

We couldn't get near the stage for the crowd that had built up, waiting for Diver to speak. On the outskirts, where we stood, people jostled to get a better look, but the closer you went, the quieter they became. Some of the townsfolk, noting the Strangers we were with, made room and we used this to head to the edge of the square. Pretty soon we found ourselves on the raised porch of one of the town houses, stood in front of the owner's bench, with a good view over the heads of the crowd to the stage.

Slake nudged Dale and pointed off to the right and we both looked over. Saxon and the Marshall stood apart from the crowd, watching Diver. The Stranger turned and looked back at us, raising a hand in greeting.

"I still think this is a mistake, my friend," Dale said.

"Noted," Slake replied.

"Friends!" shouted Diver, drawing everyone's attention. "Thank you, thank you all for coming. I am overjoyed to see so many of you here, willing to listen to my words, to hear of the one, true god."

"He may have changed his religion but he still sounds the same," Cross said. "Add a bit about Strangers being evil and it'll be no different."

"Who's the Stranger with him?" Dale asked. "Anyone recognise him?"

None of them did and neither me nor Pa knew who he was either. As Diver spoke, exhorting the powers and generosity of his god – whom he had still not named for the crowd – the Stranger stood and watched the people. His head turned from side to side, the hood still not revealing his face, as he scanned the Natives before him. His hands were clasped in front of him and hidden in black gloves. Everything he wore was black: his boots, jeans, shirt and jacket, even the gun belt around his waist, both his holsters and, from what I could see, even the metal of his pistols. The only bit of colour about him was the brass of his bullets.

"Well he's either a very nasty piece of work, or he thinks he is," Dale said.

"Speaking of which," Slake said, pointing off to the side.

At the back of the crowd, behind Diver and the unknown Stranger, three riders had entered the square. Two men, both tall in the saddle, flanked a short woman. The man on the left had his face obscured by shadow cast by his wide brimmed hat; his long, leather duster coat hid his whole body and was spread out over his ride's haunches. The other man was dressed in similar fashion but one thing made him stand out instantly: a mane of unruly hair, as white as bone, hung over his shoulders and down his back.

It was the woman between them that caught my eye – not because she was attractive – but because of the jacket she wore. The army jackets of the Kingdom of Aym were distinctive and seeing one on a short, female Stranger allowed both Pa and me to know who we were looking at.

"The Ivory Gang," Pa said. "This whole thing just gets better and better."

"Seems resurrection's quite common in these parts. I could have sworn we shot the hell out of Hook not so long ago," Dale said.

"Hook the one with the white hair?" Pa asked, obviously thinking back to the wanted posters he'd seen in the Sheriff's office over the Seasons. The Ivory Gang hadn't been down our way before, but we knew of them.

"That's him," Dale said. "It was Hook that killed our young friend here," he said, indicating Justice.

"I guess we shouldn't be surprised," Justice said. "If I can come back, why not him?"

All the while, Diver had continued to preach to the crowd. I'd only been paying half an ear to him what with talking with the Strangers and everything, but had heard the townsfolk's' reactions. They'd laughed, clapped and cheered at the start as many of them had gleefully told of how their prayers had been answered over night. Even Big Ritchie from the bar had turned up and – I'd heard this – had shouted out that he was now "the best damned piano player in the Mainland Kingdoms," In the last few minutes, though, the crowd had fallen quiet, paying close attention to the Reverend's words.

". . . but answering prayers is not all my lord will do for you," Diver called to the assembly. "He has many abilities, as many powers as he has names."

"What is his name?" several people in the crowd shouted.

"Here we go," Slake muttered, rolling himself a jay.

"He is the Start and the Finish, the First and Last in Line. He is All Points and One, Locus and Loci. He is the Northern Light and the Southern Cross, Star Shine in the Day and a Rainbow in the Night. He is the Beholder and the Watched, Seen and Unseen. He is the Man in the Silver Mountain and wants you to join him there," Diver reached into his jacket and pulled out a small, black leather book.

"This is his book, his word that I speak as he bade me do. While I call and rouse, he himself whispers softly, singing forgotten songs that will remind you of your childhood. I will not lie to you: he wants you to think of your youth. He will gather the young ones, you people, remade in your youth, and they will make us strong, all of us.

"Your prayers have been answered and always will be, but Locus and Loci, the Beginner and Ender, wants you to reach above your simple dreams of pleasure," he paused for the briefest of moments and pointed directly at Ivory and her companions. "He can give life to those who died!" he cried.

"With his help, if you look beyond your own home-grown horizons, you too can perform such feats. Come with me tomorrow; leave this town and travel East to the Silver Mountain;

meet my lord and let him become yours."

To my surprise, most of the Natives in the crowd cheered, taken in by Diver's words. They called out questions of when and how they would go.

"Let us leave tomorrow, at this time," Diver said. "Do not fear the walk to the mountains. Though they are far to the East, past the Frontiers, our lord will make the distance seem as nothing. Locus and Loci, Beginning and End, there is no middle. We need only to start our journey for it to end. Will you come with me tomorrow?"

Almost as one the crowd shouted "Yes!"

"Will you come to meet my lord?"

"Yes!"

"And will you let him be yours?"

"Yes!"

"Tomorrow, then! A new life begins for all tomorrow!"

The crowd cheered, whistled and clapped as Diver left the platform followed by the Stranger in black. Many of them headed for Diver, determined to shake his hand, congratulate him or even bow before him. Pa and I shared a look that saddened us both; we hadn't thought our neighbours so gullible.

"What's wrong, Slake?" Cross asked. The Stranger was staring at the crowd, a frown on his face.

"I was expecting someone to stand up to him. Someone to speak against him," he said. "I've heard of this happening before in other places, but a woman always speaks out against Loci's herald."

We all watched the thinning crowd milling around, many people following Diver back to wherever he was staying.

"Doesn't seem likely now," Cross said.

Someone in the crowd shouted in anger and as I looked over I saw a young man fall to the ground, out of the way of Ivory's horse. She and her companions rode through the square, forcing people to make way as they headed in our general direction. As the others noticed them, we all straightened up – except Justice who leaned against one of the porch supports – and held our hands near our guns.

For a moment, I thought they would pass by without noticing us, but the second man obviously said something to Ivory and pointed at us. She in turn said something to Hook and they all angled their horses towards us.

"Well I'll be damned," Ivory said as the three of them reined in before us. "Unbe-fucking-lievable. I couldn't believe my fucking eyes when Hook turned up less dead than we'd left him and now we run into you looking all hale and fucking hearty," she said to Justice. "Is there some weird shit in the fucking water or what?"

"Hey kid," Hook said to Justice. "Looks like we both got better. You're not going to hold a grudge about me killing you, are you?" Up close I could see he wore a patchy beard as white as his hair giving him the impression of being a lot older than he was.

"No, no hard feelings, Hook," Justice said, sounding bored.

"You speak for yourself, boy," the second man said. "I'm guessing you're the sons of bitches that shot at us from the convent," he said, looking at the other Strangers on the porch.

"And if we'd been better shots we wouldn't be having this little chat, Rune," Dale said before looking at Hook. "Although I guess even that's not a definite any more."

Pa stepped forward and placed both hands on the porch's wooden railing, leaning over it toward Ivory and her gang.

"I'm the Station Master of Cable. I've heard of each of you and know you have something of a reputation. Long and short of it is, you piss about in my Station, I'll have your asses thrown out so fast you'll think you never stopped here. You keep out of trouble and you can stay as long as you need. We clear?"

"As crystal, kind sir," Ivory said with a smile that lit up her face. I had to admit, despite the worrying number of men she'd killed, she was an awfully attractive woman. "Any chance of you pointing out where your wondrous Station is?"

"I'll come with you and sign you in, get your horses seen to," Pa said. He turned to me. "Curtis, you and your friends here might want to find Saxon and his friend, let them know we have guests."

I nodded, understanding what he meant. For all his tough talk, Pa knew that with a Marshall in town he had a better chance of being able to carry out his threats if he needed to.

He stepped down from the porch and walked off to the Station.

"See you later, boys," Ivory said. She, Hook and Rune turned their horses and followed Pa.

"Looks like you're an honorary – " Dale began as he turned to look at Cross. She, however, had eased herself into the corner of the porch and knelt down, leaving her mostly hidden by the bench and the shade. With the rest of us between her and Ivory and her gang, it seemed she hadn't been seen.

"Cross? You okay?" Dale asked. She looked up at him with such a look of rage he actually stepped back.

"Hook," she said through clenched teeth, tears running from her eyes.

"Shit," Dale said quietly, rubbing his forehead. "I'd kinda forgotten about that," Confused as I was, I thought it best not to pry into things right now. "What are you going to do?"

Cross stood up, rubbing at her eyes.

"I'm going to kill that son of a bitch. If he comes back to life again, then I'll kill him again."

We waited till Ivory and her friends were out of sight before Slake split us up so we could find Saxon and the Marshall. Dale and Cross headed out into the town while myself, Slake and Justice walked to the Sheriff's office. I didn't see the sense in splitting up until Slake explained what had happened in the town of Anchorhead.

"Them pair have gotten kinda close," Slake said of Dale and Cross. "She might benefit from having some time away from all this craziness."

"So what's it feel like? Having gods and insane Strangers mad at you?" I asked Slake, trying to lighten the mood.

"Just like old times," he said.

It didn't take too long to reach the Sheriff's office. Before we entered, I glanced over at the Station but everything seemed quiet. Ivory's horses weren't out front so they must have stabled them already. I hoped Pa knew what he was doing, fronting up to those Strangers, but I knew he had enough experience to cope. Sheriff Freewood greeted us as we walked in to the large, open office. Two of his three deputies were sat at a table playing cards and both greeted me by name. Over the years, Pa and I had often had dealings with all of them and had gotten to know them well.

"Are Saxon or the Marshall around?" Slake asked.

Freewood scratched at the slight paunch that had built up in the years since he'd turned forty.

"Saxon headed out again. Both him and Marshall Connor came back from the Preacher's sermon not long back, but he went back out soon after. Mayhap he's over at the Station?"

"What about the Marshall?"

"We've given her a room upstairs. Dixon?" he called to one of the deputies. "Head up there and give Marshall Connor a knock. Tell her she's got company."

We hung around while Dixon went to fetch the Marshall, me and the Sheriff swapping the time of day, catching up with each other's families. The other deputy, a young woman called Rand, kept glancing over at Slake and Justice with barely concealed suspicion. Despite most of the townsfolk being good hearted people, as I've said, there were more than a few who held age-old prejudices.

Dixon returned a moment or two later with the Marshall in tow.

"Afternoon, Marshall," I said. "Any chance we could have a word?"

"Sure," she said. She took her hat and coat from the stand in

162

the corner and put them both on. "Bar?"

The four of us said our goodbyes to the Sheriff and the deputies – Rand merely grunting in reply – and headed out towards the bar. There were still pockets of people standing around and as we passed them, we caught snatches of conversation. Just about all of them mentioned Reverend Diver or something he'd said. Walking past one group, I distinctly heard Emily Horse-Runner, a half-Native, half-Walker woman who worked at the large hotel in town, say that she wouldn't be going to work today.

"If we're all off to meet the Man in the Silver Mountain tomorrow, where's the need for working today?" she asked her friends. Far as I could tell, none of them disagreed with her.

"You're going to hear a lot of that," Marshall Connor said when I commented on it. "Loci draws his power from the belief of his worshippers. He'll drain this town, taking what he wants and leaving it a husk."

"Is this something else Saxon's god told you?" I asked. We reached the bar and walked through the bat-wing doors.

"R'lyeh speaks to me each night as he has done since I . . . since I first saw him."

"That must come in handy."

"No, no it doesn't," she said as we got to the bar. "He only speaks to me in nightmares."

I bought a round of drinks and we took them over to a table. The bar was busier than normal for early afternoon and most tables were full; as happened last night, though, a couple of Strangers with a Marshall was enough to secure us a seat.

"So what did you want to talk about?" the Marshall asked, sipping at her beer.

"We noticed a few other Strangers come into town while Diver was preaching," Slake said. "Ivory, Rune and Hook."

The Marshall sighed. "Great. Before all this madness started, I was actually looking for them. Now I guess there's more important things I need to deal with."

163

"You're a King's Marshall," I said. "If you don't arrest Ivory and her friends there's no telling what'll happen. They've killed plenty of Natives who've done nothing; just gunned them down for no reason."

The Marshall indicated the townsfolk in the bar.

"You think these people are worried about a couple of new Strangers? They're all convinced a new god is coming to take them away tomorrow. They don't care and neither do I."

I turned to Slake and Justice for support.

"So you're going to do nothing?" Justice asked.

"No, I'm going to try and kill their god to be rid of the one in my head," she threw her hat on the table and ran both hands through her short hair, scratching at her scalp. "The bastard won't shut up; he comes to me at night, black and glistening, tentacles flailing at me, his mouths slavering and lipless." She closed her eyes and rubbed at them with the heels of her hands. "And all day he whispers in my head, telling me to kill this Loci, this god who threatens the Land."

She looked at us, her eyes red and watering.

"I have a god in my head telling me to kill another one and it's driving me mad."

"Do you know how to kill Loci?" Slake asked, making the Marshall laugh.

"That's the messed up thing: I don't have a clue. R'lyeh keeps telling me to kill him, but won't tell me how." She waved her hand at the people in the bar again. "None of these people know what their new god's going to do with them, and if I tell them, they wouldn't believe me." She took a gulp of her beer.

"I'm sorry, Marshall," I said. Regardless of whether I believed R'lyeh was talking to her, she was clearly distressed.

"Forget it. Unless I can find a way to kill Loci it's not going to matter anyway."

Someone started playing the piano, a soft, mournful melody the like of which I'd never heard. Sat at the old upright, Big Ritchie ran his hands over the keys, filling the bar with music that made everyone fall quiet and turn to stare.

Big Ritchie played, the tune reaching out to all of us. For me, though I'd never heard its like before, it brought to mind my mother. I didn't have that many memories of her – I was just a boy when the fever claimed her – but the music made me think of her. I recalled vague impressions: love; warmth; the smell of her freshly washed hair. It made me smile at first, but I quickly realised how hard things had been without her, for both Pa and me. I started to think of stronger, clearer memories: the crystal clear image of her laying dead in her bed, Doc Valentine unable to save her; the funeral with the Judan preacher intoning over her shroud; the sight of her being lowered by a rope around her neck into the grave; the long Seasons watching my Pa drink himself into a stupor night after night.

"Ritchie," one of the men in the bar said softly. "Ritchie, stop. Please." His voice was thick and unsteady as tears streamed down his face to nestle in the stubble of his beard.

I looked around the room and most everyone seemed to be crying, each of them staring with sad, moist eyes at the piano player.

"Please stop, Ritchie," Mrs Baker asked from where she sat. A volunteer worker, she gladly gave her time to anyone who asked and never had a bad word passed her lips. She was always happy, praising Judas in almost every breath for the good life she had. Yet now she sat along with the rest of us, wretched and miserable, brought low by her memories and this music which Ritchie continued to play.

Slake, dry-eyed and unmoved, stood up and went to the piano. He leaned down and pulled Big Ritchie's hands away from the keys, bringing the music to an end. Ritchie looked up at him through his own tears.

"I couldn't stop," he said. "I was playing so well, I couldn't stop."

The doors of the bar swung open and, as I wiped my eyes, I saw Dale and Cross step inside. They glanced around for a moment before Dale spotted us.

"Slake?" he called. I pointed over to the piano.

"What is it?" Slake asked him as he walked over.

"You need to see this," Dale paused, noticing everyone's teary eyed stare. "Maybe you all do."

Slake, followed by myself, Justice and the Marshall, walked out of the bar after Dale and Cross. A handful of the townsfolk came out into the street and looked South with us, down Main Street.

Past the town's edge that was marked by a waist high picket fence, the plains and scrubland continued for miles. In the distance, a thick high cloud of dust had been raised; at the base of it was a dark line that moved and undulated though details were difficult to make out. Above it, the sky had darkened, bulbous clouds rolling forward, blotting out the blue.

"What is it?" someone asked from behind us.

"Something's coming to call," Slake said.

"It's the End," the Marshall said quietly. "R'lyeh's telling me it's the End. Death and darkness; they're rushing towards us."

"Where's the Reverend?" one of the townsfolk asked. "He'll save us. Loci will save us."

Justice turned around and spoke to the people.

"Don't you realise?" he asked, pointing out to the growing storm. "That is Loci, and he's not coming to save you."

The townspeople were silent, looking from him to the storm and back again. One by one, they began to leave, some to their homes, others back to the bar, spreading the word.

Movement over at the Station's porch caught my eye and I saw my Pa step out into the street, followed by Ivory and her gang. All along the street, people were coming out of their houses and staring South.

Pa, followed by the Strangers, headed over to us, glancing at the storm as they came.

"What is it?" Pa asked us.

"The Marshall reckons it's the end of everything," Slake said. He turned slightly and looked at Cross. She stood staring at the dark line that moved towards us, deliberately ignoring Hook.

"Marshall, huh?" Ivory said with that brilliant smile of hers. "You gonna try and arrest us, bitch?"

"I think we've got bigger things to deal with right now," Marshall Connor said, not even looking at her.

Despite her words, we all stood just watching whatever it was head towards us. Behind and around us, more and more people were moving, calling to each other, pointing South to the darkness. We heard Diver's name mentioned several times as people looked for answers.

"Would you just stand there and wait for death to reach you?"

We turned to see Saxon standing in the road. The hood of his jacket was pulled up, partially obscuring his face, and in one hand he held a large iron staff, the top of which – fashioned to look something like a castle – was marked and pitted with rust.

"Saxon? That you?" Hook asked. He stepped forward and took Saxon's hand, clasping his forearm.

"Reunions will have to wait," Saxon said. "Diver is gathering everyone in the town square. We should go there."

He turned and strode off, the base of his staff digging divots in the road. Slowly, the rest of the Strangers followed, neither gang wishing to be in front of the other. They strung out in a rough line, forcing their way through the Natives that were now filling the streets, all of us heading to the square.

Slake moved over to where the Marshall walked next to me.

"Marshall, what's your first name?"

"What the hell's that got to do with anything?"

"Your name, Marshall, what is it?"

"Samantha."

"Any other names? Second or third names?"

"No, just Samantha."

"The name Judith mean anything to you?"

"Not a damn thing. Why the sudden fascination with my name, Slake?"

"I've heard the story of Loci and his herald before and was

told that there's always a woman who speaks out against the herald. Whoever she is, Loci always calls her Judith and once he's taken as many Natives as he can, he always sends her someplace else and makes her forget what happened."

"And what about that?" the Marshall asked, pointing back over her shoulder. "What happens to the darkness that's heading for us?"

Slake shook his head. "I don't know. I've not heard of that before."

The Marshall sighed and kept on walking.

By the time we reached the town square, the Reverend Diver was already back on the stage, the Stranger in black behind him. The crowd that had formed cried out for guidance and help time and again, but Diver stood still, his head bowed, seemingly in thought.

Above us, the sky began to darken as the storm clouds rushed in overhead. The wind picked up, flapping our coats and sending more than one hat flying across the square.

"What the hell is this supposed to achieve?" Hook asked as we watched the silent preacher. "Why don't we just get our horses and get out of here?"

"No, Hook," Saxon said, turning to face him. "For good or ill, we see it through to the end."

"I thought I'd missed you, Saxon," Hook said. "Now I remember why we stopped hanging around together: you're a pompous ass."

"And you're a son of a bitch," Dale said. "Now shut the hell up."

Pa came over, jostling through the crowd of people that had followed us into the square, closing off any retreat.

"Curtis, I've got a bad feeling about this."

"You and me both, Pa. I think I agree with Hook. I think coming here might have been a bad idea."

"My dear friends!" Diver suddenly shouted from the stage. At his words, the skies opened, large, heavy rain drops spattering on to us, drumming on our hats, soaking us almost instantly. "So dear friends," he shouted again. "The end of all things is upon us, but do not fear. Did I not say that the Man in the Silver Mountain would save you? Did I not say that my god who is Loci and Locus, One Point and All, the Eastern Mountains and the Western Depths . . . did I not say he would keep you from harm?"

"What about the storm?" someone in the crowd shouted over the wind and rain.

"What about the darkness?" another cried.

"Is it an army? What do we do?" more voices shouted.

"It is an army, my friends, an army that comes to take a bite out of the world, a bite the size of Cable. But do not fear! My god has come unto you early to save you because he loves you and does not want you to fall to the teeth and claws of darkness."

The crowd shouted again, asking where this god was.

"He is among you even now," Diver shouted. He was soaked through to the skin, his hair plastered to his skull, his clothes clinging to him, but still his energy was boundless. "Though death approaches, my god has come to you to help you, but first he asks one favour, a boon of you good people."

"What? What does he want?" the crowd shouted. I realised, looking around at them, that they seemed to be comprised of the same people who – barely an hour before – were content to do nothing but wait for Loci's arrival.

"He wants your faith, your belief," Diver shouted. The Stranger in black stood behind him, unmoving, uncaring in the rain. "There are two churches in town, one of the Cuckoo God, one of Judas Christ. As your death and destruction roll closer, where are those gods? They have abandoned you to your fate, but my god, the Start and End, the Mote and Beam, my god will save you here and now, this very day. All you have to do is destroy those churches."

The crowd paused for just a moment before a yell went up and the townsfolk, some of whom I'd known all my life, turned and headed out of the square.

"Slake!" Justice shouted. "The church! I need to get to the church!"

"What are you on about kid?"

The crowd surged around us, pushing and shoving, splitting us up.

"Dale!" I heard Cross shout. I turned, trying to find her, but she was gone.

"Slake, I need to get to the Judan church!" Justice shouted over the rain and the crowd. He pushed his way through the people, half carried along by them, and grabbed both Slake's arm and mine. "I thought there'd be more time! I need to get to the church!" he shouted again.

Around us, the crowd yelled and screamed, some in fear or pain, others crying out for friends or loved ones, most shouting in anger as they headed for one church or another. A rumble of thunder overhead and the now torrential downpour combined with the voices, almost deafening us. I heard my name called but couldn't see my Pa, the afternoon sun having been stolen by the dark storm.

"Where are the others?" Slake shouted.

"I don't know, but we need to get to the church or it's not going to matter anyway."

Slake looked up at the stage where Diver still stood, crying out for the churches to be torn down. It took a moment to realise in the failing light that the Stranger in black had left.

Slake turned to me. "Lead us to the church of Judas."

We moved through the thinning crowd, me in the lead, both Slake and Justice holding on to my arms. As the Judan church was the nearest, most people seemed to be heading there so our journey was actually aided by the mob. We pushed and pulled back along Main Street before everyone surged left by the bar. The road, called William Street, was narrower, forcing everyone closer still. At the end of the street, through the rain and the gloom, a flickering light could just be seen above the crowd. It

170

took a few moments to work out that it was the church, the interior already ablaze.

"It's on fire!" I shouted over my shoulder.

"Keep going!" Justice shouted back.

We pushed and shoved through the oddly jubilant crowd. Ahead, it seemed the closer we came to the church, the more the fire took hold. Once convinced the flames were holding, a large part of the crowd headed away down another street, no doubt rushing to do the same thing to the church of the Cuckoo God. Those that were left looked on at their handiwork, some with undisguised pride, one or two with tears mingling with the rain.

"Make way! Make way!" I shouted as the crowd began to thin, the three of us eventually coming to the foot of the dozen steps leading up to the church door. The steps were flanked on either side by stone plinths, the top of each were about four feet off the ground. On each one was a stylised metal tree representing the Elder Tree that Judas Christ had been hanged from. The priest of the church, Father Cassidy, hung from the tree on our left, his hands tied behind his back, his feet barely touching the top of the plinth.

"Father!" Justice shouted. He and I ran up the stairs and on to the plinth, Justice undoing the Father's own ceremonial noose that the crowd had hung him with.

"Leave him!" more than one person in the crowd shouted.

"Leave him or we won't be saved!" another cried.

Slake drew both his pistols and aimed them at the Natives, backing his way up the steps as we managed to free Father Cassidy. The old man coughed and gasped, his face a dark, bruised purple. Behind us, the fire in the church began to really take hold and we could feel the heat radiating through the walls. Steam rose from the building as the rain boiled away.

"Diver told you to destroy the church, not kill the priest," Slake said. "You've done your work, now be on your way."

"The priest must die!"

"Kill him!"

"Kill them all!"

A man darted forward and took the first three steps in a single bound before Slake fired once, shooting him in the face. The bullet hit to the side of his left eye, his cheek and temple erupting with blood for a second before he fell to the ground.

"Get out. Now," Slake said to the others who, one by one, began to drift away.

Beside me, Justice was gently slapping the Father's cheeks, trying to make him concentrate on his words.

"Where is it, Father? Where did you hide it?"

The priest coughed again, his breath wheezing in and out of his bruised throat. His eyes bulged in their sockets, the whites having turned red from the burst blood vessels. The rain fell on to his upturned face, filling his mouth as he tried to speak.

"Altar," he said. "Beneath . . . altar."

Justice stood and, before Slake or I could stop him, dived through the doors into the blazing church. On the floor beside me, Father Cassidy coughed and retched again, blood speckling his lips before the rain washed it away. He clutched at his throat, his eyes wide, as he struggled for breath, before dying, his chest falling, his hands slipping away to the side.

With a satisfied nod, the last of the rioters who had remained turned and ran to join the others.

Slake and I stepped over to the doors, shielding our eyes from the glare of the fire, so bright after the unnatural darkness of the storm. Neither of us could see Justice.

Above us, the church groaned, the blaze eating through the timbers, weakening the structure.

"What do we do?" I shouted to Slake.

"Move!" Slake said, pushing me out of the way as Justice barrelled through the doors, his wet clothes steaming in the heat. He fell to the floor, coughing and gasping.

"Kid? You alright?" Slake asked. Justice pushed himself up on to his knees with one hand, the other clasped to his chest. In it, he held a cloth parcel, about three feet long, charred and blackened in places.

"I'm fine," he said, coughing again. "Loci's not the only god who answers prayers." We hunkered down beside him as he unwrapped the cloth to reveal a short sword. Slake took it and held it up. In the light of the burning church we could see it was old, rusted in one or two places, but still serviceable.

"What is it?" I asked.

"The Sword of Fate," he said. "As Judas hung from the Elder Tree, one of the soldiers used this sword to stab him. R'lyeh may be talking to the Marshal, but Christ spoke to me. When I was in the Station, just after I got here, Judas told me this was here and that I'd need it. If it has killed one god, it can kill another."

A gunshot tore out of the darkness and Justice's head snapped back, his hat blowing off in a burst of blood and bone. He fell backwards, the top of his head open to the elements, his brains leaking out on to the wet floor.

The Stranger in black, who had been behind Diver while he had been preaching, stepped forward, a black pistol in each gloved hand, aimed at Slake and myself.

"I mean really, is this any time for a discussion about religion?" he asked with a laugh. He pushed his hood back, exposing his face for the first time; thin and deeply lined, wearing the same big grin as the last time I'd seen him, was the jester, Loci. Up close, in the light of the burning church, I could see the leather of his jacket was made up of neat diamond shaped patches sewn together. Unlike his jester's outfit, however, they were either black or a very, very dark grey.

"I did tell you to get your Strangers gone, now didn't I, Curtis?" he asked.

Slake and I stood, the Stranger trying to hide the Sword of Fate from the jester.

"I'd be much obliged if you'd gently toss that pig-sticker off to one side, friend," the jester said, however. "I ain't a hundred percent about it being what our young friend thought it was, but I don't see no need to take a risk."

Slake hesitated for a moment before dropping the sword.

"Now you two fine gents can either move away and find something to amuse yourselves with elsewhere, or I can kill you now and save you the suspense. Your choice."

"Figure we'll take our chances elsewhere," Slake said. We moved down the steps, leaving Justice's body next to the priest's.

The jester shrugged. "No skin off my nose, boys. Dare say I'll catch up to you later." He watched us as we moved away, his guns still aimed at us as he climbed the steps. Both Slake and I walked backwards, keeping our eyes on him, and he waved at us before bending down, picking up the sword and slipping it into his belt.

"Always bet on the undergod, boys!" he shouted to us and then simply vanished, leaving only a loud clap as the air closed in on where he'd been.

"Come on," Slake said. "We need to find the others."

"What about Justice?"

"The kid's dead. Again. Nothing we can do for him now."

The church gave a groan and, as we watched, part of the roof fell in, flames rushing up to meet the storm.

Deciding that most of the other townsfolk would already have destroyed the church of the Cuckoo God, we made our way back to the Station.

"I'm glad you're okay, son," Pa said as we walked in, shaking the rain from ourselves. A fire had been lit and the room stank of drying clothes. At one table, Dale and Cross sat, holding hands and talking quietly; they both nodded to us. At another table, Ivory, Rune and Hook were sat together, each of them surly and quiet.

"Where's Justice?" Pa asked.

"Dead," Slake answered, staring at Hook. "Turns out Diver's Stranger in black is actually Loci. Justice thought he could use something against him but it didn't pan out." He turned back to Pa. "Where's Saxon? Marshall Connor?"

"No-one's seen them since the town square," Pa said. From outside, even over the sound of the storm, shouts and screams

174

were heard. Slake and I went to the window and saw Natives hurling burning torches into the houses further up the street.

"The townsfolk have lost their minds," Pa said, watching his neighbours destroying the town. We looked to our right, to the end of Main Street and saw that, beneath the storm clouds, the undulating darkness had now reached the town limits. Whatever it was, it stretched out to either side of the Southern gate.

"If you're looking at the black wall, we can tell you it goes round the whole damn town," Hook said.

"How do you know?" I asked.

"How the fuck do you think?" Ivory sneered. "You might want to be heroes, but we tried to get the fuck out of here."

"We left the square, grabbed some horses and tried to get out," Hook said. "Didn't work; that damn thing has circled the whole town and I'll be damned if I'm riding into it."

"Dale, Cross: we need to find the Marshall. She's convinced Saxon's god can help us against Loci. It's all we've got at the moment," Slake said.

"No problem," Dale said as they both stood. "We could do with getting out of here, anyway."

"What, you don't like our company?" Ivory said with a laugh.

"That's exactly it," Cross said, looking at Hook.

"Have we met before?" he asked her. "My memory's not so good since I came back," It was hard to tell if he was being serious or not.

Before Cross could say anything, Dale gently pushed her over to where we stood at the door.

"Curtis? We could use your help," Slake said.

"Sure."

Slake turned to the other three Strangers who still sat at their table.

"This whole place is heading up shit creek fast," he told them. "You know we could do with some help, but I'm not about to beg you. Help if you want or stay here and look out for yourselves. Your choice."

Rune sat back in his chair, stretching out his long legs. He looked up at Slake and smiled as Ivory smiled at him.

"Stay here and keep an eye on things, Pa," I said. "Running round in the rain's no good for an old man like you."

He leaned over the counter and hugged me, telling me to take care. With a last glance at the Ivory Gang, we stepped out on to the porch.

In the gloom of the storm, it was easy to see that things had gone from bad to worse. Patches of red and orange flame could be seen above the rooftops, illuminating the otherwise dark bellies of the clouds. After destroying the churches, it appeared some of the Natives had continued on their rampage; several small groups holding torches made of table and chair legs or chucks of wood torn from houses ran through the streets. Thick smoke struggled to rise up against the rain which, at least, had eased from torrential to a downpour. The effect was a cloying mist blowing through the town, obscuring our sight occasionally and making it hard to breathe.

"Where to?" Dale asked.

"Back to the town square. Hopefully the Marshall will think the same."

We moved off, sticking to the wooden walkways as much as we could to avoid the mud and gravel swamp that the road had become. We had no choice but to use it at one point when we approached one of the houses the rioters had set alight; flames billowed out of the windows and door, forcing us into Main Street. As we approached the bar, we found that it was also on fire, the whole of the upper floor ablaze. From within, though, came the sound of singing and Big Ritchie playing – extremely well it had to be said – the piano. We all swapped the same look, debating whether to go in and tell them. For myself, I thought they knew what was happening and that this was how they wanted things to end. After a moment's hesitation, we continued on to the square.

By the time we got there, it seemed everybody else had had the same idea. Dozens of people stood in the pouring rain, listening to

Diver who still stood on the platform, preaching to his heart's content. Loci, the Stranger in black, was not behind him.

"Can you see the Marshall?" Dale asked me. I shook my head. "Any sign of Saxon, then?" When I said no, he swore. "This is the second time we've been looking for that son of a bitch."

"What?"

"Long time ago, doesn't matter," he said and I remembered Slake had said something similar. The four of us milled around, standing on tip-toe to see over the head of other people. Clouds of smoke blew in from burning buildings, soaking into our wet clothes, muddying our faces, and over the rain and thunder, Diver kept preaching.

"I am the way, the road that never ends, I can take you anywhere! My god, he who even now walks amongst you, will give you everlasting life this very day! No longer will you be shackled to this world of anger and pain for I will take it into myself and bear your burdens! I will become your darkness, your anger, your pain! My god has allowed me to master your fears and madness; the evil voices that sing songs in your mind will bow unto me!"

The crowd shouted and cheered at his words, seemingly oblivious to the storm above them and the imprisoning wall of darkness surrounding them.

"Charlatan! Prophet of a false god!" The shout from somewhere in the crowd was accompanied by a burst of light that blazed from the top of Saxon's iron staff. The Stranger held his staff in both hands above his head and leapt the eight feet to the top of the stage. As he landed next to Diver, he brought the staff down, the glowing end leaving a trail in the gloom.

Diver darted to one side and the metal smashed into the wood of the stage sending up a shower of rain water and splinters.

The crowd roared again, this time in anger, and swelled towards the stage. Shots rang out and I saw sparks explode in the air around Saxon as the bullets hit whatever guard he had conjured around himself. This only enraged the crowd further

177

and those who could not get to the simple steps that lead up to the stage began clambering up its sides.

"Should we help him?" Cross asked.

Slake shrugged. "I think he can take care of himself. We need to find the Marshall, though."

Diver grabbed Saxon and shouted something which was lost to the rain and the crowd. The Stranger punched the preacher hard in the face, sending him staggering back. He hefted the staff once more but before he could strike, the crowd climbed up and swamped both him and Diver.

The stage creaked and snapped with the weight and finally collapsed, sending everyone crashing into the fountain it had been built over. Diver and Saxon were lost beneath the surging crowd, the light from Saxon's staff guttering and then going out.

"That's such a shame. A good herald is never easy to come by."

We turned around to find Loci, the Stranger in black, watching the scene of the collapsed stage. His arms were crossed and he wore an insincere look of sadness on his face.

Each of us drew our pistols, levelling them at him.

"Oh come now. Is that any way to treat the new god of the Land?" he asked. He shook his head. "Fire if you must, but you already know it's not going to hurt me."

"Where's the Sword?" Slake asked. I glanced at Loci's belt and, sure enough, the Sword of Fate was missing.

"Like I said, I'm not certain it wasn't the real thing so I decided to leave it back at my home in the Mountain."

"You've been all the way to the Eastern mountains and back?" Dale asked.

Loci shrugged. "When you're a god with this much power," he spread his arms wide, indicating the storm, the darkness, the still fighting townspeople. "There's not much I can't do."

"How are you at dying?"

It was his turn to spin round. Marshall Connor stood behind him, her long duster coat open and flapping in the wind. Behind us, at the fountain, the crowd had quietened down and a quick look over my shoulder showed most of them were watching us.

"Judith?" Loci asked. "Is that you?"

"I have no idea who you think I am," the Marshall said.

"I do," Cross said.

Loci turned back to face us again as Cross fired her pistols again and again until they were both empty. The jester shook and juddered as each bullet punched into his chest, tearing holes in his clothes and skin. Blood poured from the wounds, as black as sin and he looked at Cross in surprise.

"Judith?" he gasped, dropping to his knees in the mud. "But . . . I love you."

Behind him, Marshall Connor screamed, throwing her head back. The front of her shirt rippled and bulged obscenely for a moment before it tore apart.

"Don't look!" Slake shouted, clamping his hand over my eyes. I caught the briefest glimpse of thick, dark green tentacles bursting forth before I turned away. The crowd behind us shrieked as one and scattered.

The wet, slapping sounds of something huge squirming across the ground was hideous, its laboured breathing accompanying the guttural sounds of what might have been some sort of speech. Whatever the thing was, whether it was R'lyeh himself or some minion, it reached the jester who began screaming, cries that were drowned out, muffled as the thing consumed him.

As I stood, facing the other way, towards the fountain, something behind me burst with a loud pop, sending a thick mass of viscous liquid pouring around our feet. Carefully, Slake looked round and, as he stood up straight, the rest of us did as well.

The remains of Loci, the Beginner and Ender, All Points and One, were nothing more than a few scraps of torn and dissolving black leather. Not even his guns or belt had survived; whatever had burst out of the Marshall had consumed everything and then dispersed itself.

The Marshall herself lay dead in a crumpled heap, the entirety of her torso ripped open and empty.

Townsfolk ran blindly about, screaming almost constantly; several times they would run into each other or the ruins of the stage, and fall into the mud. It would have been funny if they hadn't gouged out their own eyes.

The rain eased off quickly, stopping altogether in just a few minutes. Above us, the clouds began to break up, late afternoon sunlight leeching through. Over the rooftops, at the edges of the town, we could see no trace of the darkness that had hemmed everyone in.

"Mind telling us what that was all about?" Slake asked Cross.

"My name's not Cross," she said. "Nor was it really Emma Tidyman. It's Judith." She poked at the remains of the jester with her foot. "For a long time, Loci was my husband."

"Excuse me?" Dale said.

She smiled at him. "Sorry, Dale, for misleading you. All of you. When you knew me as Emma or Cross, I had no memory of who I was. Me, the Judith part of me, only really became aware a few moments ago when Loci appeared and made himself known to me."

"I'm confused to say the least," Dale said.

"A long time ago, more Seasons than anyone can count, Loci and I were husband and wife, god and goddess. We had a . . . disagreement and he banished me to live as a Native in the Land until his herald and he would arrive to lead the people astray. It was my task to prevent that if I could."

"So why didn't you do that here?" Slake asked.

"Because for the very first time, I was a Stranger. The story had changed and when I didn't challenge Loci's herald, he knew he could do more than steal people away."

"So all this –" I said, pointing to the madmen and women, the still burning buildings, the body of the Marshall. "– all of this is your fault."

Cross, or Judith as she was now, bowed her head.

"It is partly my responsibility, yes. But by breaking the story, I broke Loci's control over it and me. For the first time, he didn't

180

know how it was going to end. Despite his claims, R'lyeh could not kill him. Only I could, and only when he reminded me of who I am."

"So what now?" Dale asked.

Judith sighed and stepped away from the gently bubbling mass that had been, apparently, her ex-husband.

"I have to go, if only to ensure there are no others left in the Mountain."

"So that's it?" Dale asked. "You're just going to walk away from all this? From me?"

"Who said anything about walking?" she said, smiling the same lop-sided smile that Loci had used. She vanished, the air rushing in to fill the space she'd left. Just like Loci.

Slake, Dale and myself stood looking at the two empty footprints.

"That's it," Dale said, wiping at his eyes, smearing the dirt over his face. "I give up. No more. Women and religion. Forget them both." He rubbed at his eyes, blinking back tears and swore.

"Come on, let's get back to the Station," Slake said.

"What about this?" I asked, pointing to the remains of Loci. "What about the Marshall? Or these poor bastards?" I waved at the lunatics who were still running and screaming, blood thick on their faces, their empty eye sockets torn and ragged.

Slake shrugged. "Sorry, Curtis. We helped you with Diver. That was the deal," he said and headed off down Main Street. A moment later, Dale followed him.

"Deal? You son of a bitch. You Strangers are as bad as she is," I shouted. "Causing all this shit and then just moving on, leaving us Natives to sort it all out."

"Heard it all before, Curtis," Slake called back to me.

I watched them walk, their heads low. Slowly, I followed them.

Several of the houses on Main Street, as well as the bar, were now husks, still ablaze, sending plumes of dark smoke into the now mostly clear sky. The Station hadn't been touched,

181

thankfully, and as we approached, we found Ivory and her two compatriots readying their horses.

"So did the good guys win?" she asked us.

"No thanks to you," Slake said.

"Not my fight," she said simply, stepping up to the much taller Stranger. "Want to make it mine?"

Behind her, Rune came out from behind his horse, a hand on his pistol. Hook hung around at the back.

Slake and Ivory stared at each other for a moment.

"See you around," Slake said and stepped up on to the Station's porch. Ivory and the others climbed up on to their horses and, as I passed her, she winked at me.

We all stood on the porch, watching them saunter off, all three of them looking over their shoulders at us, Rune and Ivory grinning broadly.

Slake opened the Station door and walked in.

"Curtis!" he shouted. Both Dale and I rushed inside.

My Pa was splayed out on one of the tables, his chest soaked in blood, at least half a dozen bullet wounds in him.

"Bitch!" I hissed and rushed back outside.

The Ivory Gang were halfway up Main Street, still looking over their shoulders and laughing as they rode. I started running after them, hearing Dale and Slake hit the wet ground behind me then following. I drew my pistol, shooting and yelling at them as they kicked their horses into a trot.

A figure could be glimpsed at the end of Main Street, clutching a large staff. He held it aloft and a sheet of flame sprung from the buildings on both sides, meeting in the middle and soaring upwards.

Ivory and Rune reined in their horses who reared up, terrified by the flames. Only Hook spurred his onwards and leapt through the fire.

The moment's hesitation was all we needed. I stood in the street and calmly aimed at Ivory, tracking her bucking mount with my pistol. Just behind me, Dale and Slake stood, both with guns drawn.

"Damn you," I whispered and fired, shooting not Ivory but her horse, the Strangers behind me opening up as well.

Ivory's horse fell to the ground, pinning her to the street. Rune screamed her name, drew both his pistols and fired on us. We fired back and one or more of us caught him, a couple of times in the chest. He fell backwards in his saddle and his horse bolted, carrying his corpse South into the plains.

I walked over to where Ivory lay, her leg crushed beneath her horse. She sobbed uncontrollably as she lay in the mud.

"My leg. My fucking leg," she moaned. She looked up at me. "You shot my fucking horse."

"You shot my Pa," I said, brought my pistol up and shot her in the head.

The wall of fire burnt out and Saxon came down Main Street, leaning heavily on his staff. He was bloodied and bruised, one eye swollen shut and short a couple of teeth.

"Diver's dead," he said as he neared me. "He shall preach no more."

I turned and walked with him, breaking into a run when I saw Dale kneeling in the road with Slake. As we approached, Dale stood, letting his friend fall back, two gunshot wounds in his chest.

"He's dead," Dale said. "Hook?" he asked Saxon.

"He got past me. It was all I could do to maintain the fire."

Dale nodded. He rubbed at his eyes again, clearing the tears and dirt away, looking down at Slake's body.

"What now?" I asked, looking around at the devastated town, its inhabitants dead or mad, its buildings burning and deserted.

Dale reached down to Slake's body and pulled his gun belt free, slinging it over his shoulder.

"I'm sorry about your Pa, Curtis," Dale said. "He was a good man." He clapped me on the shoulder and walked back to the Station.

"That's it? You're just going to leave?" I called after him.

"I too must be on my way," Saxon said. "Great R'lyeh never sleeps and already calls me to attend him.," He placed his hand on my shoulder. "Be strong," he said, hefted his staff and walked away.

I stood in the middle of Main Street, a gun in my hand and a dead Stranger at my feet.

After I buried my Pa in the graveyard, next to my Ma's grave, there didn't seem much point staying in Cable. Most everyone who survived the coming of Loci started drifting away, quietly leaving the dead and the mad to fend for themselves.

I packed up what I needed and rode North to Jerusalem. I made a report to the Marshall's office – Sheriff Freewood was one of those who had died so I thought it fell to me – and set about making a life for myself.

As the Seasons went by, I thought less and less about that whole time. I met a woman, Jennifer, and settled down with her. She was a widow with two grown up sons and we all got along just fine.

I stayed clear of the two Stations in the city, wanting nothing more to do with Strangers.

A couple of years down the road and things were good: I had a wife I loved and who loved me; I had a job and some savings; I had a life that was quiet.

One evening, leaving a bar called The Juggler's Rest, I heard someone call my name.

I turned and, from the alley that ran down the side of the bar, a woman stepped out. She wore a long green skirt that reached the dusty ground but was spotless. A dark red bodice was pulled tight at her waist, her bosom swelling above it. Her hair was long and curled, a dark brown shot through with lighter streaks and it framed her pretty face where a lopsided smile sat on her lips.

"Hello Curtis," Judith said. She looked much the same as she did when she was the Stranger, Cross. A little fuller in the body and face, and perhaps a little younger, but it was her.

"What do you want?" I asked her.

184

"It's been a long time since Cable, hasn't it?" she said. "But I've been thinking about what you said, about that whole episode being my responsibility, my fault."

"It's taken you two years to think about that?"

She frowned at me and, I swear, there was the sound of thunder overhead.

"I'm allowing you a degree of familiarity, Curtis. Don't think you can overstep the mark, however," she straightened her skirt and smiled again, that same lop-sided smile I'd seen before. "I accept some responsibility for what happened in Cable, and for the actions of my late ex-husband. In order to make it up to you, I'd like to offer you a job."

"A job?" I asked, not really sure this was happening.

"That's right. Putting things right at the Silver Mountain took a lot longer than I expected. I freed the few remaining souls Loci had left there, but now that's done, I find myself in a strange situation. No-one has heard of me in such a long time, you see. No-one really believes in me any more, except the few I freed, so I need someone to spread the word," She looked me in the eye, still smiling.

"I need a Herald, Curtis."

"And you thought of me? Why?"

"You have been touched by the gods, Curtis," Judith said as if it were the most obvious thing in the world. "You have been in the presence of three of this Land's greatest gods. Who better to tell my story of how I was betrayed, how I suffered and ultimately regained my godhood?"

I was stunned, I really was.

"You want me to find believers for you? To tell your story? You helped destroy my home town, allowed my Pa to be killed and you want my help?" I said, angry at her arrogance.

"Careful, Curtis," she said, and again there came the sound of thunder. "I'm offering you the chance of a lifetime. The opportunity to leave all this behind and live with me, as Herald to a god."

I stepped forward and, for the briefest moment, almost lashed

185

out at her. I stopped, however, and just looked at her in disgust.

"I want nothing to do with you and your kind," I said. "You bring nothing but misery."

"Don't turn this down, Curtis," she called after me as I turned and walked away, heading home. "It's a once only offer."

I ignored her and kept walking.

"Fine. As soon as I have a Herald, I'm making this place my first stop. I'll do to Jerusalem what Loci did to Cable. I will bring forth the same darkness as he did and this time I'll unleash it on the Land."

I stopped and looked back at her, smiling my own lop-sided smile.

"And how will you do that if no-one believes in you?" I asked her. "Without followers you're nothing. You may as well not exist."

I turned and walked away, listening to a god begging for my belief.

Also Available from www.pendragonpress.net, any bookshop

(ISBN 9781906864248; £9.99)

Or, via scanning the book's QR code with your smart-phone: